DOUGLAS WILSON
BLACKTHORN WINTER

DOUGLAS WILSON

BLACKTHORN
WINTER

1250 Belle Meade Drive
Lancaster, PA 17601
800-922-5082

First Edition 2003

Copyright © 2003 Veritas Press
1250 Belle Mead Drive
Lancaster, PA 17601
ISBN 1-932168-10-9

Paintings by Peter Bentley

Printed in the United States of America.

For Rory Douglas Wilson.
May you always defeat the pirates.

CONTENTS

FASCINATION

Anumber of years ago, probably when your grandfather was a little boy, there was another young boy named Jim Monroe who lived alone with his mother. Her name was Sandra, and she was by nature a very pleasant woman. But even so, because of her circumstances, she was harried and somewhat distracted. A few years before our story begins, her husband had been killed in the Korean War, and she was left to provide for and bring up her son and manage the small remains of a once-large estate. But that requires more of an explanation, and so I suppose I shall have to give one.

Because of the nature of the story I would like to tell you, I cannot say exactly where they lived, but since the story itself will give some things away, I can tell you that it was somewhere in the Tidewater area of southern Maryland or northern Virginia. Beyond this, I am afraid I have to ask you not to be too curious.

Honesty also requires that I tell you that I have changed around the names of some of the towns and rivers I mention just to help you not be more curious than you should be. So if you have done well in your geography lessons, you will notice some inconsistencies in the following descriptions.

But though I have told you not to be, Jim was curious, and that is why I have such an interesting story to tell you. He was not curious about everything, but on a few subjects you have probably not met a more curious boy. His brown eyes were deep and inquisitive, and when it grew long enough to see, he had dark hair. Jim had a pleasant nature, like his mother, but I have to say that he was quite a bit more adventurous. One of the things that fascinated his curious heart more than anything else was the whole subject of pirates. Whenever he had a free moment, his thoughts would drift naturally and easily back to his favorite pirate caves and coves, pirate treasures, pirate battles and crimes, and of course to the great pirate captains. He did not admire them at all, but they did thrill him. On rainy afternoons especially, he would seek out his favorite books to read and reread some of the stories.

You may think that this was just a short enthusiasm. Young boys often have such great interests that only last for a short time and then fall away as soon as they are distracted by another one. But Jim loved his pirate stories faithfully. The interest had come upon him one day in the previous school year, when his teacher, Miss Robinson, had mentioned in passing that the great pirate Blackbeard had once landed several miles from where the school was, and a very short way from his house.

Up to that point, Jim had known a number of pirate stories, just as all boys do, but they had all been "simply stories." He had thought of them the same way you might think about *Treasure Island*, as an exciting story that could never happen anywhere, to anyone. But for some reason, the fact that Blackbeard had landed on the banks of a creek just down the road from his house made everything very close and very real, and for the first time an interest in pirates seized Jim by the throat. What used to be remote and distant was now ever present in his imagination. That very afternoon, Jim had checked a book out of the library on Blackbeard. And when he lay in bed reading that night, he came to the story of how Lieutenant Maynard had sailed against Blackbeard down in Caroline and fought a glorious battle with him, bringing the pirate's head back to Virginia hanging from the bowsprit of his ship. Jim set the book carefully down on the floor beside the bed, turned out the light, and for the next several hours he had been too excited to sleep.

Your grandfather and Jim almost certainly never met, but they may have lived in the same kind of house. Jim and his mother lived in a grand old house that the family had built around the turn of the century. It was red colonial brick, but the style was too sturdy and close to the ground to be considered in the colonial style. Though this house was built around 1910, the Monroe family had actually been living somewhere on the same property since the early eighteenth century. The Monroes had once been very well-to-do, but this was sadly not the case now. This is where the "remains of an estate" I mentioned earlier come in. In the very

early years, the Monroes had been wealthy, but the family fortunes had declined markedly after the War Between the States. Even so, they still maintained a respectable place in the community for quite a long time, and when Jim had been born, the estate still had several hundred acres. But after Jim's father had died in the war, the various taxes they had to pay had imposed a horrible burden, and his mother was forced to sell off some of that acreage. But even this did not end their financial troubles.

Because she could only work part-time, Jim's mother had not been able to keep up on the property taxes for so much land—they owned about fifty acres still, down to an inlet south of their home. Sandra sometimes felt that it would be far easier to just sell everything and buy a house in town—but when she reflected on the fact that Jim was the last of the family with the name Monroe, and that the family had been on this land for hundreds of years, she kept trying to work out a way to stay. She had not been born a Monroe, and she did not feel right making that kind of decision for Jim. When he was grown, he could move away if he wanted, but she did not want the responsibility of trying to explain to him why she had not kept their land. And so she determined to remain until there were no choices left.

Their property taxes had been in arrears for several years, and they had another court date scheduled in several weeks' time. The judge had said at the last hearing that he was very sorry, but that if payment of five thousand dollars was not made to the county clerk by the next hearing, then the government would have to take direct action to collect their back taxes. And that meant seizure of the property, she was sure. The judge had said he was sorry, but Sandra didn't think he looked sorry. His name was Jonas Beard, and he was a very important man in their small community—he now served as judge, and before that he had spent many years on the school board. But for all his apparent public spirit, he was still a puffy and self-important man.

There were no relatives to help them, and no one to borrow money from. But one day, Sandra had an idea. The attic contained a few notable family heirlooms, objects she would never part with. But the attic also contained much older furniture, significant to no one, but which might attract the attention of antique dealers. So she decided to have a sale and emptied most of the furniture out of the attic down into the garage. The dark wood attic now seemed enormous and very dusty, and it somehow looked older and far less familiar than it had been before.

When they had cleared everything out, Jim and his mother found a trunk of old books in a back corner. Most of them were history books, but there were also a few books of theology and some old grammars. Sandra gave Jim the job of sorting out any books that he might want, and to set the others aside for the sale. And that is how Jim found the old letter in the attic on a very rainy day. On both ends of the attic, small windows opened up to a gray sky, and Jim did not know why, but all of it seemed very appropriate.

As he rummaged through the box, the title of one book caught his attention immediately. It was called *A General History of Pirates* by a Captain Robert Johnson. The date of publication was 1852, but the book had been written a century before that. The pages on the side had that rough cut which old books sometimes have. Jim started to read through it, and felt the familiar lump of excitement well up in his throat. But then he remembered he had a job to do, and reluctantly set the book aside to take down to his room later. But as he did so, he noticed a piece of paper sticking out the side, near the back of the book. At first he thought it was one of the rough cut pages that had come loose. But when he looked closer, and opened the volume again, he saw that it was an old letter.

He gently opened it. There were five or six pages to it, and the paper was water stained and yellow. The paper creaked when it opened it, and Jim had to handle it gingerly. In places, the ink was smudged by the water but fortunately most of it was legible. It took him a few moments to figure out who had written the letter and who had received it. But the date on it was 1935, and the name of the recipient was Leonard, and the one who had written it was your "affectionate grandfather." Jim's father's name was Leonard. There were no last names anywhere. For all Jim could assume at that moment, it was just an old newsy letter to his father that would make his mother cry. But even so, before he read a word of it, he knew that it was far more important than this. When he thought about the moment of discovery later, he concluded that his knowledge came from a combination of the gray sky, the pirate book the letter was in, and the desperate circumstances he and his mother were in. "It was just a pirate kind of day," he explained to me later.

So it was probably a letter to his father, written when his father was a boy, and it was written to him by his grandfather. The letter was telling him how the family fortune had been made back in the first part of the seventeen hundreds. And it had been quite a fortune. "Dear Leonard . . ." the letter began.

But of course, now I have to back up for a moment. This letter that Jim found certainly did not contain everything that I am about to tell you. But the letter did lead to a number of other discoveries, and during the course of these discoveries, many other interesting facts came to light. For example, Jim's mother remembered some things her father-in-law had once said, things she had not understood at the time. She also found some interesting written comments made in some old family histories and genealogies. And a few of the family members in the early years had even been important enough to have had biographies written about them, and Sandra carefully read through them, trying to piece things together. Jim, for his part, not only had found the letter in the book, but also was able to contribute what he knew about pirates. And he also played a very important role later on, which I will have to tell you about when we get to that place in the story.

So, though I suppose I could tell you the story as it came out for them, in dribs and drabs, I do not think that is really the best way to do it. Although it was very exciting for them at the time, it would be very poor story-telling on my part indeed. And so I have decided to tell you all the facts as they looked once they were finally sorted out and placed in a proper order.

I suppose I should introduce myself as well. I was a friend of Jim's father in the war, and after the war, I looked in on Sandra and Jim from time to time to see how they were getting on. At first I did this because of my friendship with Leonard, and a sense of duty I suppose. But as time went on I found that I had a keen interest in Sandra. But all that had already started some time before this adventure started. Nevertheless, because of it, I was close enough to the whole thing to be able to tell you the details of the story. And so I suppose I had better get to it now.

A Very Idle Boy

THOMAS INGLE WALKED SLOWLY DOWN THE STREET. The year was 1705, the third year of the reign of good Queen Anne, and Thomas was now fifteen years old. He had been born in the second year of the reign of King William and Queen Mary, and he had grown so quickly he was almost ready to go out into the world. But the world was already very different from the one he had entered just a short time before.

Just like Jim Monroe, he lived alone with his mother, who supported them both by working as a day servant in the home of a wealthy tobacco merchant, a man named John Hutchins, who was a friend of the governor. Tom's father had been lost at sea five years earlier—whether to a storm or to pirates, no one knew. All they knew was that his ship had left the mouth of the Chesapeake in late spring, and that it had never arrived in England.

Thomas had stayed at home to finish his schooling, at the insistence of his mother. He had asked her many times if he could apprentice himself as a ship's boy, and she had always said, "Someday, Tom. But you must master your books first." And so he had worked hard, but felt badly because he was doing nothing to support his mother. She was only able to make about ten pounds of tobacco a day—tobacco was the currency in those days—and so they lived at a very modest level indeed. Thomas would tell her often that when he could go to sea, he would soon enough make their fortunes, and he would then come back, and they could buy a small farm. Land was not that expensive, but it was still beyond their means, and there was even more money to be spent in setting up a farm. She was glad for his desire to work in order to help, but warned him more than once that fortunes are not obtained just by going to sea, and that words on their own can't fill a bucket. Once he had pressed the point, and she had said, "Mere wishes are silly fishes." She was always saying things like that.

Thomas was a well-built boy, and handsome in appearance, as his mother told him once. He had sandy, blond hair, which was tied off in the back. His breeches and shirt were home-spun, but well-kept up for all that. But his shoes were old and tattered, and the buckles on them were starting to come off. Shoes were expensive, and after his lessons were done every day, Thomas used to spend many hours walking along the creek banks and in the woods, thinking and dreaming about the sea. His mother had told him not to be so hard on his shoes, but it was difficult for Thomas to walk without being hard on them.

As he walked down the street, Thomas suddenly stopped in order to listen to a commotion that was taking place in the shop he had just passed. He turned around just in time to see a young man tumble headlong down the front steps of the candlemaker's shop—that candlemaker being one Mr. Jos. Whidby, as it read on his sign. He was a small, rotund man, but he was energetic, hardworking and strong. These were all characteristics that made him most impatient with his apprentice, Isaac Taylor—the young man who was now lying on the street at Thomas' feet. Mr. Whidby stood in the doorway of his shop with puffed out cheeks, which were purple and unused to this uncharacteristic temper. He then clambered down the steps, pulled Isaac to his feet, boxed his right ear, and said, "There! That's to send you off with! Tell your father that your apprenticeship is over, that you are a lazy no-account of a boy, and that if he wants to settle the money with me, he may come see me at his leisure." With that, Mr. Whidby hit him on the side of the head again, turned abruptly, and stumped up the stairs and back to his candles. Most of the time, he was a jolly and pleasant man. Thomas heard him muttering as he went back into his shop, "It could rain porridge, and he'd have lost his bowl!" The door slammed tight.

Isaac just stood there for a moment, rubbing his ear. He had a shock of disheveled brown curly hair, puffy lips, and an unpleasant complexion. Thomas did not like him, but he also felt sorry for him sometimes.

"What did you do, Isaac?"

Isaac looked up startled. "Oh, hullo, Thomas." He continued to rub his ear.

"What did you do?"

"I was just resting and thinking. Mr. Whidby seems to care more about his candles than important things."

Thomas knew Isaac to be a very idle young man, and so he said nothing. They started to walk down the street together.

"My father told me that if this apprenticeship failed, then I had to make my own way. I can't go home now." Thomas knew that Isaac was seventeen, and that it was long past the time for him to be out in the world, and so he nodded silently. Mr. Taylor had tried three times before to set Isaac up in an apprenticeship, and now this was the fourth failure. So then Thomas asked, "What are you going to do?"

"That is what I was thinking about when Mr. Whidby interrupted me. I didn't like making candles. Who wants to make dumb candles? I am going to make my fortune, and I am not going to do it the way these stupid shopkeepers do, a penny a day. I met some gentlemen at the Oar and Compass last week, and they invited me to come to sea with them."

"Oar and Compass? Isaac, those men were pirates and villains! Governor Seymour sent word to the tavern and ran them off."

"Pah!" Isaac puffed his lips out further. "The governor here is hot and unhappy, just like Mr. Whidby. But these same men have dined with the governor down in Caroline. They are just gentlemen of fortune. And they have been most welcome in Pennsylvania."

"Isaac, they are not gentlemen at all. They are buccaneers. If you go with them, you risk swinging."

"All I know is that they have their fortune. You should have seen how they bought drinks for everyone, out of a sack of pieces of eight.

They were generous and full of adventure. Not like Mr. Whidby. And besides, Thomas, nobody really knows what a pirate is. Some folks call them pirates, but lots of them are privateers. And most everybody buys things from them sometimes—even Mr. Whidby did once."

"That's different," Thomas said. "When the king says you can't buy things you need from anyplace but England, and England doesn't send it to you, and the pirates have it, I don't think there is anything wrong with it."

Isaac snorted, "Thomas, when you are as old as me, you'll know better. If it isn't wrong to be with the buyers, why would it be wrong to be with the sellers?"

"Because the sellers are murdering pirates! They kill people— they probably murdered my father."

Isaac decided against arguing the point, and the two walked down the street together. After a few moments, Isaac spoke again. "I am going to go home—I have to get a few things. And I can say farewell to my mother before my father comes home."

Thomas decided to try a different approach, but he had to think for a moment about how to do it. He had to appeal to Isaac's laziness without calling him lazy. "Isaac, the pirates aren't going to make you first mate when you get there. You'll have to do a lot of work you don't like. It'll be worse than Mr. Whidby. And my mother says that fair dealing brings wealth slowly."

Isaac shook his head. "Yes, slowly. You didn't talk to them, Thomas. These men know how to live. You should have seen them. I'm sure they will have a good place for me. Thomas, they invited me! I need some adventuring. It will be good for me." But Thomas thought to himself, "If an ass goes traveling, he'll not come back a horse." So he decided to stop arguing. "And when I come back," Isaac said, "the first thing I am going to do is take one of my gold pieces, go back to Mr. Whidby's shop, and buy me a candle!"

Thomas told his mother about Isaac that night. Sarah Ingle was a very pretty woman, about thirty-three years old. Like many women in that day, she had had a case of the pox when she was younger, but it had barely left any scars at all. Unless she told you about it, which she was not likely to do, you wouldn't know there were any scars. But still Thomas knew she was sensitive about it, and that she thought it was the reason she had not married again.

Thomas and his mother had two rooms off the back of one of the town's thriving inns, a place called Reynold's Inn. The owner and his wife felt sorry for them, and so they charged a very reasonable rent, and in exchange, Sarah Ingle helped in the inn during busy times when she could, and Thomas sometimes helped with the horses.

Thomas had a cot in one of the rooms, and his mother had a bed, slightly nicer, in the other. In addition to the cot, Thomas' room had a small table, where he kept his few things, and his books. He was working through his last book now, a primer on navigation. His mother's room had a small, writing desk, and a bookshelf where

she kept her Bible, her prayer book, and her copy of Baxter's
Everlasting Rest.

When Thomas had first gotten home that night, his mother was
not there. He looked at the shelf, and her prayer book was gone, so he
knew she was across the street at St. Anne's. She would often go there
for a few moments of quiet after her day of work. He waited, and
after about ten minutes, she came in, and he told her about Isaac.

"It doesn't surprise me," Sarah Ingle said. "A cask savors of its
first fill. He has always been a very idle boy—and he always brags
of many goodmorrows."

"Mother, I don't know how he thinks he can find the pirates again."

"Mr. Hutchins said today that the pirates didn't leave the colony,
but just moved down the coast toward Virginia. They are just
taunting the new governor. I am sure they know the king's frigate is
at the northern end of the bay. Sure, Isaac can find them quickly
enough. He probably has enough money to take him that far."

"Should we talk to Mr. Taylor?"

Mrs. Ingle shook her head. "No. We have nothing to say to him.
Isaac is a lazy boy who wants to be rich. Mr. Taylor is the same way,
only a little less lazy. If Isaac was a dog, he'd lean his head against the
wall to bark. We can pray that God has mercy on Isaac's soul, and
that he learns from the pirates what he could not learn at home."

"How can he learn anything good from pirates?"

"He might learn that he doesn't belong there. And he might learn
that Mr. Whidby is a wise and kind man."

"Still," Thomas said, "I feel sorry for Mrs. Taylor."

"The pirates are a wicked lot, and I feel sorry for Mrs. Taylor too. She married unwisely, and her son is a fool like her husband—he has a bone in his arm and so cannot work. But even so, there is still hope for Isaac. And, leaving the pirates out of it, there is only one thing worse than a boy who leaves home," she said, "and that is a boy who doesn't."

At these words, Thomas knew it was time to ask his mother again. He took a deep breath and held it for a moment. "Mother, I am almost done with my last book, the one on navigation. May I go down to the docks tomorrow and speak with Mr. Jenkins?" Mr. Jenkins was a harbor merchant they knew and trusted in the parish, and he would know which captains would be good to apprentice with, and he could give Thomas a letter recommending him. He owned a warehouse down by the harbor, and he had dealt with most of the men who sailed the Chesapeake for many years. He knew which were honest, and which were not, which obtained their goods by trade, and which by piracy, and which were harsh with their crews, and which were wise.

Sarah Ingle was quiet for many minutes. Thomas knew that something was different, because whenever he had asked before, she always said no right away. "Thomas, you know that the Ingle men have always gone to sea. I have known since you were born that you would go to sea—you were bred to the sea, and you have the bent of your father's bow. But I lost your father there, and I do not want to lose you there." With this her eyes filled up with tears. "I am very sorry, Thomas. I wasn't going to cry. Yes, you may talk to Mr. Jenkins."

Thomas didn't know what to do. He had a lump at the top of his chest in sympathy with his mother, but his stomach was churning with excitement. So he just sat where was. After a few moments, he thanked his mother, took her hand in his, and promised her he would come home safely.

"I won't require it," she said, "but I would prefer that you ship with someone who trades with Jamaica or Bermuda, instead of England. That way you will be home more often, and I will know how it is with you."

"Yes, ma'am," he said.

"And promise me that you will stay away from rum and bawdy houses."

"Yes, ma'am," he said.

"And we will have to buy you a prayer book to take with you."

"Yes, ma'am."

"And I hope the cold I feel in my bones is just the cold of late April. I hope this is just my blackthorn winter." Thomas was silent.

THE MULBERRY TREE

THOMAS HAD NOT BEEN ABLE TO SPEAK with Mr. Jenkins
for two days after his mother had given him permission. On
the first day, Mr. Jenkins was too occupied in business, and on the
second he was home ill. But on the third, Thomas presented himself
to the merchant and made his request.

Mr. Jenkins rubbed the back of his neck. He was a grim but
kindly man who had left Edinburgh ten years before. He had been
a faithful covenanter in his days there, but everything was different
on the Chesapeake, and so he was willing to offer his own form of
dissenting worship at St. Anne's. Still, he was completely unrepen-
tant about his past and had once told Thomas some stories about
the killing times that had filled Thomas with a mixture of horror
and delight. Once when the rector at St. Anne's had mentioned those
days in a sermon (with his Anglican view of them), Mr. Jenkins had

walked past Thomas after services, muttering and shaking his head angrily. "Ye kin call a sheep's tail a leg, but that don't help him to walk. Murder is murder for a' that."

But now Thomas was standing in his warehouse, holding his hat nervously in front of him. "So, ye want to go to sea, lad. Tis a good thing—I was starting to wonder about ye. Aye, I can give ye a letter— your mother is a good woman—and I can tell ye who to take it to. The *Prudent Hannah* is due to return from Jamaica in about a month. Her captain is John Monroe."

Thomas was thrilled. "I might be able to go to sea in a month?"

"Naht s' quick, laddie. The *Prudent Hannah* is due to be careened, and Captain Monroe told me she needs many repairs beyond that. But once that is done, he wants to get in one more Caribee voyage before winter."

Thomas was grinning widely, and so Mr. Jenkins glowered in his kindly way. "But I can only recommend ye, I can't add you to his crew. He is a good man, but he is a stickler for work. He will probably have you work for him in port before he takes you in his crew."

"I can work," Thomas said eagerly.

"Nah duut," the Scotsman said.

With the prospect of going to sea looming before him, Thomas finished the navigation book with a will, and then tried to fill his days doing odd jobs at Reynold's Inn. But there was not much for him to do, and so he took to filling his afternoons by taking long walks. He knew he would miss that when he finally got to go to sea.

One afternoon, he was a number of miles south of town, and he stood alone at the end of a small inlet off the Severn River. He glanced at the sun, and estimated that he needed to start walking home soon. The inlet gradually worked its way toward the solid ground by means of a marshy strip, covered with cattails. Thomas quietly stood in thought, throwing bits of stick into the water. The day was quiet, and although it was summer, it was not too humid. The green trees around the inlet hovered over the face of the water, and reflected a deep green all around the edge of the water.

Suddenly, a bowsprit appeared to the left, out in the river, belonging to a small sloop coming upriver. He didn't know why, but Thomas quickly stepped back into the trees. There was a sharp hill behind him, and Thomas scrambled quickly up the hill. He remembered a good view of the inlet from the top when he was walking down. This was an isolated area—no inhabitants for miles north or south, and any ship like this was as likely to be a pirate ship as not. I need to make myself scarce, Thomas thought.

Thomas stood quietly at the top of the hill and watched as the small sloop hove into the inlet, and dropped anchor. After about fifteen minutes, a shoreboat was lowered from the side, and three men got in it. Two of them began rowing straight in Thomas' direction, while the other sat in the stern looking intently at a package in his hands.

The boat disappeared from his view, and Thomas looked around. Near the top of the hill was a gigantic wild mulberry tree.

Thomas could have escaped detection easily by heading inland but by now he was very curious. He decided to stay in order to find out what they were doing, and to climb the mulberry tree to avoid being discovered. It was a good climbing tree, and Thomas was able to get high up in its branches. He lodged himself in a crook near the top, knowing that he was completely invisible unless they climbed up the tree too. He hoped to be able to hear what the men were doing, and possibly to catch a glimpse of them.

"Here's a big tree, lads. Can you remember this?" Thomas realized with a shock that the voices were coming from the base of his tree. There was no answer, probably because the two oarsmen just nodded. Then one of them, a different voice, spoke. "I don't like it, O'Conner. If Cap'n James finds out we're crossing him, he'll stick his gold toothpick in each of our eyes, and that would just be to start with."

"We're not crossing him." O'Conner's voice was soothing. "Leastways, not that anybody knows. This package probably ain't worth nothing—I'm just curious about it, that's all."

The other voice joined in. "I dunno, either."

"Look," O'Conner said, a little loudly. "James made us the prize crew, didn't he? He told us we could have whatever was on board, didn't he?"

"That's because he thought there wasn't nothing on board."

"Well, you two are too far in now, anyhow. You were hot for the plan a whiles ago. And James will do whatever he wants just because you came this far. Let's just bury this, and we can come back later for it. Can you remember this tree?"

Two reluctant voices replied, "Aye."

"Now, dig the hole. We have to head south so we jin up with the others there in a reasonable way. We don't want the lads thinking we sailed up to Philadelphia. If they start asking questions, you two sisters would probably tell them everything you know, which ain't much. But it would be trouble enow."

Thomas sat quietly in his crook, and listened carefully to everything. After the space of twenty minutes or so, the brief comments, grunts, and scrapings from down below stopped. "Good work on't. Let's go, lads." Thomas, looking out, could see the inlet, and there was the sloop rocking back and forth on its anchor. He could see two or three other hands moving around on deck.

Thomas waited a long time before he could see the boat again. The man named O'Conner was at his place in the stern once more, this time with his back to Thomas, and his two confederates were steadily rowing. Thomas continued to watch them, expecting nothing but to see them depart as they had come. But what he saw next filled him with horror, and almost caused him to fall out of the tree. When they were a boat length from the sloop, with one motion, O'Conner pulled two pistols from his belt and calmly shot both men at the same moment. In one instant, Thomas saw two puffs of smoke, one of the men stand and topple over the side, and the other one slump over his oar. He saw O'Conner stand and bend over the seaman still in the boat, and then he heard the dull crack of the pistol reports. He was sick at his stomach, and his hands were instantly clammy. He watched with a horrified interest as O'Conner hoisted the second oarsman up, and pushed him into the water.

He continued to stare, and O'Conner reached the ship, secured the boat, and hoisted anchor. The other sailors were apparently in on it, for they gave O'Conner a hand up as though nothing had happened. Thomas wondered vaguely how O'Conner was going to explain the loss of his two men to Captain John James. James was a notorious pirate on the Chesapeake, one who had filled the authorities with consternation more than once. Thomas watched silently as the sloop disappeared out of the inlet.

When he had climbed down from the tree, he had little difficulty in finding the place where the hole had been dug. He had no shovel to dig with, but he brushed away the leaves with his hands, and started to lift the loose dirt out with his hands as well. The hole was only about two feet deep, and at the bottom was a small oilskin package. The shallow burial either meant the contents of the hole were not important, or that O'Conner was only intending to hide the package there for a very short time. But one of these options was not a reasonable one—Thomas knew that the oilskin package at the bottom of the hole was something worth murdering two comrades for. And that meant that O'Conner would be back soon enough.

On his knees, with trembling hands, he opened the package and stared at the contents, mystified. There were two pieces of paper, one of them a folded chart. It had no peculiar markings of any kind on it, and was the kind of hand-drawn chart Thomas had seen countless times before. The other was a simple piece of paper, covered with strange ciphers. He stared at both for a few moments, but realized that this would take a great deal of study.

He stood, and started to walk away from the hole, leaving it open and empty. Then he stopped, shaking his head at his own stupidity. That would tell O'Conner that someone had seen them. If he filled the hole back in again, then O'Conner might think that one of the seamen he killed had sneaked the package out before they buried it. He went back and pushed the dirt back into the hole, and covered it over with leaves again.

As he walked home, his mind was filled with excitement. If these were pirates, and they were, and this was a map, and it was, then there was likely a treasure to be had. But O'Conner didn't seem to be sure that this was a treasure. Of course, that may just have been for show so that his two companions did not revolt. If they knew that a vast treasure was at stake, then they would no doubt panic at the prospect of crossing someone like John James. So there probably was a treasure, and then Thomas stopped walking for a moment in his excitement—he could take care of his mother. The only questions were how great the treasure was, and how to decipher the map. A moment later, he was not sure again. Maybe it was just paper.

When he got back to town, he hid the strange package in the stables behind the inn, and got ready to go have dinner with his mother. He was consumed with curiosity, but he knew that he couldn't tell his mother the story until he knew more about what was in the package, and that looking carefully at the contents of the package must wait until the next day.

He also knew that she was very likely to want him to take what he had found and turn it over to the governor's men. But that would make it public knowledge who had found it, and it would tell

O'Conner who had witnessed his murders. Maybe he shouldn't say anything at all to anybody.

Thomas knew that he had to think about it. He started to go in, and then remembered the dirt on his hands. That would require an explanation. He turned around and went back out to the stables, where he scooped water out of the trough for the horses and carefully washed his hands. He shook his hands carefully until they were dry, walked up to the back entrance of the inn, and went inside. For all the excitement, he wasn't very late.

CAPTURED!

THOMAS WAS FRUSTRATED. In the days following his adventure at the mulberry tree, he had many opportunities to study the map, and the paper that was with it, and he was in no way able to make any sense of it. Judging from the way the coastline appeared, the map seemed that it could be somewhere on the Eastern Shore of the Chesapeake, but there were many other places which could have the same kinds of inlets. None of the creeks and inlets were labeled—it was just a map of a complicated coastline. There was something strange about the coastline too, something he couldn't quite identify. For some reason, something about it did not look right or natural.

He was frustrated for another reason also. The weeks until the return of the *Prudent Hannah* went by with an aching slowness, and the humid Maryland summer made everything seem a little slower still. This gave him time to think a good deal about what he should do with his map when he went to sea. He had finally decided not to tell his mother about it, because he couldn't imagine anything they could do about the difficulty that wouldn't endanger them both. He also decided that if he figured the map out, or had any ideas on how to do something about it, that he would tell her then.

In the meantime, Thomas decided to spend the time he had until he went to sea studying the map and the paper, committing them both to memory. He would be able to hide the oilskin pouch at home easily enough, and if anything came up on his journey where he had to have the map, he would be able draw it again. And so he spent his afternoons studying, just as he had done before. He was accustomed to study, and it was not long before he had them both committed to memory. This was harder than his usual lessons had been because with this map and code he had no idea what anything meant, but it was still something he was able to do within a week's time. He then made sure of himself, reviewing the map and the strange ciphers in his mind every day, and after several weeks he was comfortable knowing that he could draw both out by hand.

Day followed day, and finally enough time had passed for Thomas to start running down to the docks every afternoon to see if the *Prudent Hannah* had arrived, or if there was any news of her. He would walk along the docks first to see what new ships had arrived, and after he was disappointed, he would go see Mr. Jenkins at his warehouse. "No news, laddie. Maybe tomorrow." And Thomas would tip his hat, and walk back up the hill toward home.

But waiting does have this reward—when the thing you are waiting for finally comes, all the hours spent waiting for it are all gathered up at once and rush to your chest, and they make it hard to breathe. At least it was this way for Thomas. One afternoon, just after he had eaten a simple lunch of oat cakes, he walked down to the docks, trying hard to expect nothing—but one of the first things he saw was a strange sloop tied up on her starboard side, with her bow pointed out to the river. He broke into a trot as soon as he saw her, and ran until he could see the name spelled out on the stern. *Prudent Hannah.*

He veered off and ran to Mr. Jenkins' warehouse, and when he arrived there, blowing a little, Mr. Jenkins smiled a grim little smile. "Here's your letter, lad. But I warned ye about the work. Captain Monroe was in here this morning lamenting his shipworms terrible like. After we are done offloading his cargo, said he, he was going down to the South River to careen his ship. But he told me he was looking for good hands—he lost some in Jamaica, and some more this morning when he docked."

Thomas took the letter, thanked Mr. Jenkins several times, and walked quickly out the wide door of the warehouse. When he got to the sloop, he stopped at the gangway, and waited nervously until the mate came over to the rail.

"Permission to come aboard?" His voice didn't quaver, for which Thomas was very grateful, but his mouth was dry, and the palms of his hands were sweaty. "Come aboard, aye," the mate said, and Thomas made his way up the gangway. He said he had a letter from Mr. Jenkins, asked to see the captain, and followed the first mate as he led the way to captain's quarters. He swallowed many times on the way there, trying to remember the things he ought to say, and hoping he wouldn't say anything stupid.

He told his mother that night that he would be going with the *Prudent Hannah* in the morning to begin working on cleaning the ship, but that they would be back in harbor within a week or so. Captain Monroe had already made arrangements with Mr. Jenkins for a full cargo of tobacco, and so they would come back to load up, and then they would sail for Jamaica. Captain Monroe had treated him politely enough, but had promised him nothing. "If you work as Mr. Jenkins says, then you may sail with me. But if you shirk, or if you stand around waiting for someone to box your ear, I'll bring you back here, and you can explain to Mr. Jenkins why you made a liar out of him."

Thomas had worked far harder than anyone expected, including himself, and was gratified after two days of it when the mate took him aside and jokingly told him not to make the other hands look bad. The work did not require any peculiar training, and once you had the hang of it, the only thing to do was work hard or not. Thomas labored away methodically until his hands blistered and bled, and he slept very well every night. Careening a ship means tilting the ship in shallow water on her heel, sharply to starboard, and repairing and caulking portions of the hull normally below the water line. The crew scrapes barnacles, cleans weeds, looks for shipworm, and caulks anything they need to with oakum and pitch. Then the whole thing is done over again, listing to port.

The only trouble Thomas had during that time was once when the first mate told him to scramble down below, into the smallest hold in the aft of the ship, and bring back a chisel the mate had left there. Thomas jumped to it, but stopped suddenly when he came to the small entry of the hold. Peering down inside, he saw that it was dark and wet, and there could scarcely be any room for turning around. Since he had been a small boy, Thomas had been deathly afraid of closed and dark spaces—his mother didn't know what to make of it, and neither did Thomas. But there it was, and here he was, needing to get a tool just a few feet away in a dark hold. He couldn't go down into the hold, and he couldn't go back and lie to the mate. Thomas just stood there for what seemed like hours to him, but it was actually just a few moments. He was breathing deeply, and the palms of his hands were clammy. Then, suddenly, like spring after winter, the mate's voice came floating over the deck. "Never ye mind, laddie! Found it in my belt!" Thomas had never heard better tidings in his life.

When the ship returned to harbor ten days later, Thomas walked up to his home, gratified at the report he could give his mother. The captain had commended him, and brought him into his crew. He knew his mother would be sad that he was going to sail, but that she would have been disappointed in an even deeper way if he had failed at his work. If he had taken on his employment as Isaac Taylor

would have, he could have come home to stay for a time, but with
no pay to give her but excuses. "Excuses make for thin soup," Sarah
had often told her son when he was little.

When they had finished their dinner that evening, Sarah Ingle
told Thomas to sit on the edge of his bed. She then disappeared into
her room, and returned carrying a very small sea chest. "I am sorry it
is so small," she said, "but it was all I could afford. Now, go on, open
it." Thomas turned the latch, lifted the lid, and inside was a change of
clothes, suitable for the sea, a pair of shoes, a few small cakes she had
made for him, and a prayer book. "Thomas," she said, "your mother
will pray for you, and so you must pray for your mother." Thomas
promised, thanked her again, and then they both sat quietly, not
knowing what to say, and not needing to say anything.

The ship pulled away from the dock at dawn. Sarah stood on the
docks, next to Mr. Jenkins, and they both waved as the sloop pulled
away from the dock. Thomas had time to wave briefly, but even
though he was an inexperienced hand, the first mate had him
scurrying around the deck, hauling in lines and coiling them. When
he was done with that, the dock was far astern, and he could not
even make out any figures on it.

Thomas could feel the swell of the water beneath his feet, and
the salt air he had breathed his whole life seemed completely

different to him now. The sloop was a smart one, and rolled evenly
beneath him, and a whiff of salt spray enchanted him. He had never
been so excited. It was a beautiful day, and the breeze off the bay
buffeted his face. He was very happy. The first mate, whose name
was Alford, came by a moment later, and said, "Come over here,
laddie." Thomas followed him curiously over to the port side of the
ship where Alford showed him the coils of line there. "Now, do these
look anything like the fouled rat nests you made over there on the
starboard side?"

"No, sir," Thomas said.

"What are you going to do about it then?"

"Ay, ay," Thomas said, and ran back over to starboard to coil the
line again. This took him about half an hour—he had to run back
and forth to see what the line was supposed to look like—and when
he was done, he reported back to the mate, who then put him to
work on a number of basic tasks. And whenever he thought he had
nothing to do, he was to holystone the deck.

Kent Island and the Choptank River were barely visible to port,
and the leagues slid swiftly beneath the keel. They were making
their way to the Virginia Capes, with the hope that they could put in
at the York River to load their final provisions of water before
making their way out to sea. Once they were past the Capes, the
captain wanted to sail clear south, not putting in anywhere,
proceeding as fast as he could. If the winds were fair, he could sell
his cargo in Jamaica and return to Annapolis by September.

Several days passed in this way, and while the weather stayed
pleasant, the chop of the waves picked up. Thomas was very grateful

that he did not appear to be sensitive to sea-sickness. Bred to the sea, his mother had said.

The *Prudent Hannah* was a small merchant sloop, and had no artillery. So, after three days, when a strange sail appeared in the distance off their port bow, Captain Monroe tacked hard to starboard. "The Eastern Shore is a true hive for sea-rovers," he muttered to himself.

"Does he mean pirates?" Thomas asked one of the other hands.

"Aye," was the reply. "Pirates, rogues, knaves, and every manner of sneaking puppy."

"All hands on deck!" The captain roared. "If he tacks to follow us, we make a run for the Patuxent. And everyone look alive."

The first mate clambered up into the rigging, glass in hand. A few moments later, he bellowed down at them, "She's coming about!!" In a moment, Captain Monroe had the crew throw every sail up, and the sloop quickly bent before a favoring breeze.

At first Captain Monroe had wanted to make the mouth of the Patuxent, although it became quickly apparent that the strange vessel would be able to head them off. But it also became evident that *Prudent Hannah* had a much shallower draught than the other ship, and so the captain changed his plan, and began hoping to take refuge among the many shoals that lined the shores of the Bay. At the captain's command, the mate had several of the crew go below and stave in the water barrels in the hope of making the draught shallower still. In desperation, he ordered the helmsmen to turn a couple of points nearer the wind. However, this run for the shoaly water was clear to the pirate captain as well, and before Thomas had much time to reflect on what was occurring, the other ship had managed to cross their bow, and fired one small swivel gun from her rail as a warning.

Captain Monroe was no coward, but he had no guns, and hence no opportunity to swing the sloop around to offer a broadside. All he had was the futility of possible musket fire, and so he ordered the boatswain to strike the colors. This was done, and the crew of the *Prudent Hannah* waited glumly for two longboats from the pirate ship to arrive. This they did soon enough. The pirate sloop was about 60 tons, and had eight guns. A blood red flag flew above her, and she was named the *Lady Constance.*

Thomas stood with the other sailors in a group, and watched in horror as the pirates strolled around the deck of the *Prudent Hannah.* Most of the crew were appalled at the simple insolence of the robbers, but Thomas had other concerns. The leader of the boarding party was O'Conner, the man who had buried the map.

One of the things pirates often did on their raids was recruit from the crews of their prizes. But Captain Monroe had picked his men well—they were all honest men, and all shook their heads when the offer to turn pirate was given to them. They knew well enough that whenever an honest man was turned from seamanly behavior, the pirates would take care to involve him quickly in some awful crime so that there would be no turning back for him, and he would come to end of his days decorating a gibbet.

The captured crew stood in a close knot on the quarterdeck, Thomas standing in the middle of them. Several of the pirates stood guard over them all, while the other pirates ran over the ship, laughing and shouting. They went alow and aloft, taking everything of value they could find—the captain's silver, eleven pipes of wine, cable, extra rigging, and some casks of rum. But the cargo itself was mostly tobacco, and the pirates did not want to be troubled transferring it to the *Lady Constance*. So it was decided to keep the sloop as a prize.

"What are they going to do with the tobacco?" Thomas asked a crewman next to him.

"There are some honest merchants on the Eastern Shore, who have more business with pirates than they should have," he answered simply. "I call them honest out of Christian charity," he added, and then was silent.

When the frenzy of pillage was over, the pirate boarding party assembled in front of the prisoners again. Thomas licked his lips nervously. He knew there was no way O'Conner would know him, but that did not change the sensation that Thomas had that he ought to know him. Thomas had watched him commit two murders, and he had a hard time imagining that O'Conner could not know the one who had seen him. But the pirate walked by Thomas several times, and took no particular notice of him.

Because the thieving was over, O'Conner beckoned to Captain Monroe to step forward.

"Have you seen what we have done?" O'Conner asked.

"I have seen the mischief," the captain replied.

"By the powers!" O'Conner said, in mock anger. "You call it mischief? We are merely small nations, and do to ships what France does to England, and England to France. Mischief! Why do you not call us patriots, instead of desperate fellows?"

Captain Monroe decided it would be futile to answer, and so he remained quiet. Besides, he had sometimes wondered the same thing himself—not that he would ever justify piracy, but he sometimes had wondered how much piracy under another guise sustained and stained the honest intercourse of Christian nations.

THE FIGHT

AFTER A PRIZE CREW HAD BEEN ASSIGNED to the *Prudent Hannah,* they were instructed to drop off Captain Monroe's crew at the closest likely place that promised a goodly walk to the nearest town. The two exceptions were Captain Monroe and Thomas, who were kept prisoner, perhaps in the hope of using them as hostages if they were overtaken in any kind of pursuit. If they were not pursued, then one of the pirates said they would probably drop the two off at the southern end of the Bay. But these two remaining prisoners were to be held over to the *Lady Constance* to be kept there until a pirate council could determine what to do with them.

Captain Monroe had his hands tied behind his back, as did Thomas. They were escorted to one of the deck guns, and were securely tied. And there they sat, as the *Lady Constance* made her way steadily south, with Captain James wanting to put as much blue water as he could between the place of robbery and where they would relax to celebrate their haul. According to all reports, although the royal frigate *H.M.S. Anne Arundel* was still far up in the northern end of the Bay, it was better to be prow southward.

Captain James strode back and forth across the deck, impatiently. He wore a bright blue coat, and he had two braces of pistols strapped around his chest. His hair was long, dark and greasy, and was tied off carelessly in the back. He had various necklaces around his neck, with one of them displaying an elegant gold toothpick. He was a quiet, intense man, and constantly scanned the Bay ahead and astern without speaking. He had the air of one who was content enough with the small sloop they had taken, but who still hoped to fly at high game.

"Why do they need a council?" Thomas whispered to Captain Monroe. "Why can't James just decide what to do with us?"

Captain Monroe just made a face. "These hardened rascals are not really under the command of James. Pirate ships are floating democracies, which is one of the reasons they are so vile. According to pirate custom, James has authority over them in the warmth of battle. In all other things, they permit him to command them as they command him to. Many pirate captains are driven before their crews, all sail and no ballast."

Thomas just sat silently for a few moments. "What will happen to us then?"

"It depends on what this crew is like when they start in with their drinking and roaring. They took six casks of rum from my hold, and I'll wager that all that rum will be off to rum heaven soon enow. As for us, it'll be more wind from the same quarter."

The *Lady Constance* sailed steadily south for five or more hours. The wind was fair, and the sky blue. The Eastern Shore was sliding by their port side, and as the sun finally began to sink, the ship soon sought out an inlet to anchor in, and settled on the lee shore of a small island there. The inlet was apparently well-known to them, and had been their destination all along. When their sails were reefed, and the anchor slid into the water, the pirates gave out a great cheer, and the casks of rum were immediately trundled out. The *Prudent Hannah* followed them into the small bay about twenty minutes later, and anchored about fifty yards away. As for the prize crew on the *Prudent Hannah*, one of their number drew the short straw, and remained on guard, while the others rowed over to join the festivities.

Several of the pirates brought out some fiddles, and began a lively tune for a jig, and the rest of the pirates began downing the rum. Thomas had never seen anyone drink that way, and so he looked on in astonishment. "They are preparing themselves to give judicious counsel to their captain," Captain Monroe said. "No rum and no fiddles would throw their government off the hinges."

"Aye," Thomas muttered.

After about an hour most of the men were in as drunken a pickle as can be imagined, and the musicians put away their instruments—apparently so that they could begin doing their part in the consumption of the rum. The noise of the gathering—all the pirates were assembled on deck—became somewhat more subdued, and one of the pirates stepped forward, and raised his cup. He was a savage figure with wild hair, and a bright red sash around his chest, looking quite the gentleman in his better blue clothes, but a noisy, surley fellow. "A gallant dog," Captain Monroe said to Thomas.

"A toast, mates!"

"A toast!" the company roared.

"Here's to our mate Hitchens, hung like a dog and sun-dried at Execution Dock, Wapping on Thames!"

The pirates roared again, "Aye!" All was quiet for a moment as they drank down the toast. But then, one after another, pirates would step forward and offer their toasts, each more gruesome and macabre than the last. Captain Monroe whispered to Thomas that he did not like how things were blowing up. "This looks like a foul wind to me," he said.

Finally, another of the pirate crew stepped forward, cup in hand, and Thomas exclaimed under his breath. "Isaac!" Isaac Taylor had not been improved by his new companions. His face was flushed from drinking, and he looked perfectly wretched. The pirates had realized from the first that he was more bluster than action, more cunning than courage, and had put him to work cooking their food and tending to the slops. And even with his apron set aside, he did not look at all like a dashing pirate. But still, he clearly wanted to be accepted as the fiercest among them, as a staunch pirate, as a great rogue.

Isaac lifted his cup. "A toast!" he cried.

"A toast!"

"To our prisoners!"

The pirates exhaled all together, "Ahhhhh . . ." Cruelty and drunkenness were mixed together in varying measures. "Carry on, cook, on with your toast," one of them shouted.

Isaac lifted his cup again, "To the young one, cut into pound pieces with a true Spanish blade!" A murmur of approval ran around the gathering. Thomas felt himself flush with anger, mixed with just a touch of fear. But the fear was small enough to ignore, while the anger was not. Here was Isaac Taylor, with the courage of a small and fairly timid squirrel, trying to . . . "Captain James!" Thomas suddenly shouted out.

"What does your rascal carcass want?"

"When you are hard at work on the high seas, plying your difficult trade, do you not from time to time seek occasion for restoring your nerves?"

The pirate captain glared at him. "I don't give time to answering riddles, I'll be bound. Tell me what you mean by shouting at me."

"I can see from your proceeding that your crew needs entertainment after a hard day at your vocation. I propose to provide it for you, if you let me fight your mess cook."

At this, Isaac Taylor turned suddenly white, and stepped back two steps. This brought a roar from the pirates, and Thomas immediately knew he would get to fight.

"Why should I let you fight one of my crew!"

"Because this one looks like he needs practice fighting. Would you feel safe taking him on a boarding party?" At this, Isaac stepped forward, leaned over and hissed quietly at Thomas. "What are you doing? We were friends."

Thomas looked up at him and loudly replied, "If your captain favors my request, I will speak with you by and by." Captain Monroe, tied up next to Thomas, was looking from one to the other with fascinated interest. Isaac quickly turned to the pirate captain. "Of course, I would fight him, but my stew . . ."

Captain James waved him off. "Hawkins, go look in on Mr. Taylor's stew. Then hurry back, lest you miss a fine fight." Turning back to Thomas, he said, "How would you like to fight?"

"I would like to fight with my hands, so that I can feel what I am doing."

Isaac's face displayed a mixture of consternation and fear. He had only known Thomas before in the context of worship at St. Anne's, and was not expecting such ferocity from him. One of the pirates came over to loosen Thomas's bonds, and when he was free he sat for a while rubbing his wrists in order to get blood back into them. While he was doing this, Captain Monroe leaned over to him. "Well executed, lad. It was looking ill for us for a time. But two cautions. You have come alongside him well, and have grappled his brains tight on the starboard side. But as you prepare to board him, remember that even a coward can fight when he has no choice."

Thomas nodded.

"And," the captain continued, "when you come to it, fight like a Christian man. Give quarter if he asks it, and don't let him make you as foolish and cruel as he is. If you learn to hate as they do, they have conquered—and they understand this, for it is how they recruit. Take your lessons on hatred from the prayer book, don't let the sun go down on it, and God bless it."

Thomas nodded again. "I thank you, sir." The warning was a good one, for Thomas was very angry. Thomas briefly wondered how the captain knew to give this advice. At this moment, Hawkins came scurrying back from the galley. "Too late, cap'n! The stew has escaped, and the kettle is cold!" At this, the pirates roared again, and Isaac flushed with embarrassment and fear.

Captain James drunkenly signaled his quartermaster, who staggered out in the middle of the deck. "Gentlemen!" he said, and the pirates shouted with laughter.

When they quieted down, he spoke again, "Do you have anything to say before we begin?" He looked at Isaac, who responded with characteristic bluster. "The devil himself should be feared of me tonight." With this comment falling cold to the deck, Isaac attempted to glare at Thomas, who simply returned the gaze. Isaac met his look for several seconds and then looked down ashamed.

"And you?" the quartermaster said.

Thomas simply said, "God bless Queen Anne."

Thomas was not really sure why Isaac was so afraid. He was taller than Thomas by four or five inches, and he was a good bit heavier. Judging from his height, Thomas guessed that he had a much longer reach as well. But Isaac was still clearly afraid.

Thomas stepped slowly toward him, and spoke softly as he came, "Isaac, you ran off to join these gentlemen of fortune, and now you are a gentleman of fortune yourself. But for such a gentleman, your excellency is extremely out at elbows. What can the reason be?"

At this, Isaac snarled and swung wildly. Thomas stepped aside easily and threw his right fist as hard as he could into Isaac's mouth.

The unfortunate boy staggered backwards, and almost fell down. The pirates all cheered loudly at the first blood, having apparently no loyalty to their own shipmate. Captain Monroe felt the same way, but for a different reason. "Smart as paint, lad," he said to himself.

Thomas followed hard after Isaac, and hit him two more times. But Isaac recovered his footing, and circled away, holding his fists up in front of him. It was settling hard upon him that he had no choice but to fight, and the fact that he could taste blood in his mouth calmed him for a moment, oddly enough. He had been hit, and he hadn't died. The strange sensation of courage was new to him, but it must also be said that it was still egg-shell thin, and lasted only a few moments. He swung at Thomas again, and this time he struck Thomas' arm, which deflected the blow. But Isaac, as a fighter of great inexperience, thought he had done some damage and crowed irrationally. For his part, Thomas just laughed and settled down to business. With dogged single-mindedness, he aimed every blow at Isaac's puffy lips, trying very hard to make them puffier. It gave him one thing to think about, one target for his labors, the one thing needful. There was only one thing in the world for Thomas, and that was Isaac's mouth.

After receiving his fifth blow, Isaac was bleeding profusely at the face, and was blinking quickly. He tried to fight on, but his eyes were quickly swelling shut, and a lifetime of laziness was making it quickly impossible for him to do anything but burst into tears. He choked these back, but was only partially successful. He had signed the piratical articles, and had sworn on a hatchet (for want of a Bible), and yet he still had no courage.

Thomas continued to pummel him, most of the blows connecting. Within a few minutes, it did not matter whether Isaac had his hands in front of him or not. Every blow was striking him with full force.

Thomas stopped for a moment, with Isaac standing helplessly in front of him. His hands were trembling, and feebly clenched in front of him. "God have mercy," Thomas said, and hit him again, harder than any blow he had delivered thus far. Isaac went down with a cry, and lying on the deck burst into a flood of tears. Lying on his back, he held out his hands for quarter.

Thomas turned away in disgust, and began to walk back to where Captain Monroe was seated. Captain James was equally disgusted with the whole affair, and shouted at Thomas as he walked past, "Lad!" Thomas stopped and turned to look at the pirate chief, who said, "On my ship, the victor has privileges. Would you want my dirk to finish with then?" With this he held out his knife, hilt first. Thomas looked back at Isaac, who belatedly understood his cruel captain's offer and crawled up onto his knees. Thomas looked at the knife, and then at Captain Monroe. He had no question in his mind about what he would do, he just thought he should look at everything as though he were thinking about it. When he had done so, he shook his head, walked back to the cannon, and held his hands behind him to be tied again.

When Thomas was tied up, Isaac recovered his feet. As much as I would like to say something different about him, the poor wretch had no understanding of himself and no shame, and so he came over to revile Thomas for betraying their friendship. Thomas just looked back up at him and said, "Isaac, you could make a cat laugh." But just then, one of the pirates, less drunk than the rest, came over and clipped Isaac on the back of the head. "The young master here declined the dirk. D'ye want me to go get it, and offer it to him again?"

Isaac shook his head. "Then back to the galley with ye. Try to find your rambling stew." With this, Isaac shuffled off into the darkness. By this time, most of the pirates had been laid out on the deck by the rum, and some were already snoring.

"I'll have to thank you," Captain Monroe said, "for saving our lives."

PIRATE HUNGER

IN THE MORNING, a brisk breeze was blowing in from the Bay, and Thomas reluctantly woke up. He had slept fitfully, hands tied behind him, and he did not like to think about how stiff he was going to be when he was finally freed from his bonds.

Captain Monroe's voice came from the other side of the gun. "I've had better berths, I must say." Thomas groaned in reply, and they both sat up slowly, and inched to the point where they could see one another.

Thomas looked across the deck, where he could see Captain James consulting with O'Conner, both of them with an intent look upon their faces. It was plain that O'Conner was trying to talk his captain into a course of action. Thomas wondered briefly if it had anything to do with the map that O'Conner had hidden at the mulberry tree. Captain Monroe looked at the two men talking and said to Thomas, "That O'Conner pirate has a head full of bees."

The two men began to walk slowly across the deck to where the two prisoners were. Their conversation was general enough for anyone to overhear—but they could not know that Thomas knew certain secrets that would make their words far more revealing than they knew.

Captain James shook his head. "I seen it done better," said he. "But as bad as old Jeffreys was, he still hid things well enow."

"Hid?"

"Once I saw him draw one in Kingston, the strangest thing that ever you saw. It looked like a shoreline drawn by a mapmaker in the drunks."

"Aye, cap'n, whatever ye say. But now you're makin' me yaw in a quartering sea."

"It was a child's trick. He made the sea the land, and the land the sea."

At these words, Thomas saw O'Conner, who was walking behind Captain James, smile. Or, as he described it later, it was more like a hungry leer. At that moment, Thomas knew that O'Conner had seen the map, and had not been able to make sense of it, any more than Thomas had been able to. The smile also told Thomas that O'Conner had not been back to the mulberry tree. Thomas closed his eyes and called the image of the map up—all the inlets and bays were actually peninsulas and points jutting out into the water, and all the fat points were creeks and inlets. And what Thomas had thought was a strange bit of shoreline on the Eastern Shore was actually a portion of the coast along the western shore of the Bay.

The pirates moved out of earshot, and continued their conversation up on the quarterdeck. Thomas kept trying to guess if Captain James now knew about the map and was conspiring with O'Conner, or if O'Conner was still hiding it from him as he had been doing when he buried it. What was apparent is that all the pirates knew the general location of the treasure, and that they were moored near the place where they thought it was. Captain James gave an order, and the crew began the work of warping the two ships further up the creek. They did this by running lines to trees along the shore, and winching themselves farther away from the mouth of the creek and the sight of any who happened to be sailing by on the Bay.

After about an hour, when this was done, a landing party began to form under O'Conner's command. It had apparently been decided that Captain James would stay with the ship, and that O'Conner would lead an expedition looking for signs of the treasure. The party was commanded to return within two days whether they had found anything or not. It was also decided that they would take Captain Monroe and Thomas with them, and release them far inland. When they asked them, Captain Monroe volunteered that he had grown up in the area, and knew it well. And of course, the pirates had no idea that Thomas knew what they were looking for.

The various members of the pirate band going ashore were all showing signs of suffering from their drinking the night before, but one of them, a man named Carter, was as surly as a butcher's dog. He had continued to drink into the early morning hours, and he was still more than half drunk. As they were walking along the path, Carter complained loudly once or twice about the pace. After the second time, O'Conner stopped the party and came back to roar in Carter's face. "When your worthless life comes to swinging, mate," he roared, "I will be the one what ordered your bag of bones triced up at the fore-yardarm!" Carter knuckled under immediately, but the rum was still with him, as well as the aftermath of the rum that had left, and he remained as surly as before.

As the party resumed walking along the path, Carter took his place behind Thomas, and in his black humor began to amuse himself by pricking at his heels with a cutlass, trying to trip him up. Occasionally, he would strike Thomas between the shoulder blades with the hilt of his cutlass. Thomas was a prisoner, and did not see there was anything for it except to manage as best he could without complaint. At the oddest times, things his mother used to say would come back to him. He bears misery best that hides it most.

They proceeded inland, along the banks of the creek, for the space of two hours and a half. The way was largely uphill, and as it was a warm morning, the men had soon broken sweat and were breathing hard. They came to a clearing where two great trees had fallen over, and O'Conner called a halt to let the men rest. The two trees were on either side of the path so that as they rested, the men were facing each other across the path. Carter was just across from Thomas, and Captain Monroe was on the other end of the same log as Carter.

"Boy!" Carter suddenly said. He had clearly taken a deep and irrational dislike to Thomas. Thomas looked up at him without saying anything.

"What's your mother's name, boy?"

"Sarah," Thomas said.

"Sarah!" Carter sneered. He then said a few vile things about her, and then glared at Thomas to see what he would say about it. Captain Monroe looked alarmed and motioned to O'Conner to intervene. O'Conner waved him off, probably because he was curious about what would happen. But the most anyone was expecting was for Thomas to take a verbal lashing. What they did not reckon on was the young man's courage, his quick wit, and the effect the two together would have on someone in as foul a frame as Carter was in, a man who was ripe for any mischief in the world.

But Thomas did not immediately answer, but just smiled grimly and looked down. Carter kept talking, loudly, and with incessant cursing and swearing, he kept on reviling Thomas, his mother, and all his ancestors. In the years after, Thomas would always say that power in mean and ignorant hands makes men wanton, and this is where he first learned that lesson deeply. Thomas could feel his gorge rising, and he knew that within a few moments there would be no looking back. Carter continued in his bitter tirade, sullen as winter. Thomas still said nothing.

"Well, boy," Carter said. He turned a quid in his mouth and spat on the ground. "I am tired of carrying this conversation by myself."

Thomas made no response.

"I said I am tired of conversing with you in this fashion, boy." Thomas still said nothing, and so Carter added, "M'be it's because I call you boy. What's your name, boy?"

Thomas looked up. "Simon," he said. "Simon Tugmutton." The rest of the pirates laughed at this, and Captain Monroe, in spite of how anxious he was, laughed in spite of himself. Carter blushed, or blushed as deeply as a black dog can, and stood to his feet.

"So you want to be saucy," he said. "I think I should make you join me in conversation."

Thomas said nothing, and just looked back at Carter. This infuriated him still further, and so he shouted, "What do you think gives you leave to look at me like that?"

"A cat may look at a king," Thomas said.

"I want you to tell me about your mother." Carter was flailing now. He did not know how to joust verbally, and he knew that he was not in control of these exchanges.

"She is a lovely woman," Thomas said. "I would prefer not to mention her in this company."

"But I require it," Carter said.

"Much I care," said Thomas. Captain Monroe looked beseechingly at O'Conner again. O'Conner shook his head.

Carter said something foul again about Sarah Ingle, and then demanded that Thomas repeat it. "I will not say it," Thomas said, "but I will say that you are as sad a rogue as ever went unhanged."

"Shiver my bones, you insolent pup! You talk to your betters this way?"

"No, I do not," Thomas said. The pirates all laughed again, and one of them shouted out to Carter, "You can't get away from him nohow, Jack!"

Carter snarled back, "And you can go hang." He was standing in the middle of the pathway now, vaporing aimlessly with his cutlass. He had expected Thomas to stand upon a defense, cornered and caught, but instead he had cut his cable and was giving him a running fight. And not only was Thomas in the right of it, but he was also getting the best of it.

Carter did not know what to do. Every time he came in close to say something, Thomas poured in a broadside. And every time he stood away, his mates laughed at him. And every time he spoke, Thomas answered defiance. To make things worse for him, Carter was not a bright fellow at noon straight up, and despite many years of trying, the rum had not helped him on this score at all. He spoke again, far more quietly, but his face was tinged with a purple anger. The effect on his speech was a low hissing. "So, you mock me, a poor sailor, sent off to sail the Main as a young boy. You mock me, and my sainted mother, who taught me psalms and the catechism." Captain Monroe, off to the side, could tell that Carter was in a very dangerous mind. He was talking off his head, acting as though Thomas were the pirate, and he an innocent orphan victim of circumstance. And only a peculiar blindness induced by a bad combination of anger and rum would make him mention his long-forgotten psalms and catechism.

The captain hoped that Thomas would remember what he had told him the night before about leaving Isaac a way of escape. But Thomas, while he knew the wisdom of this, did not yet have the patience that comes with years that would enable him to understand when he should apply that wisdom. Thomas was angry enough not to be able to see how angry and irrational Carter was.

"Whines and complaints make for a poor pudding, as my mother used to say," Thomas said.

"Your mother . . . !" Carter shouted.

"I can tell chalk from cheese," said Thomas, "and I can tell a rascal from an unfortunate sailor. And I can tell gallows bait from a quartermaster."

And with that, Carter decided to end the argument the only way he knew how. He pulled a pistol from his belt, and, before anyone had a chance to move or say anything, he leveled it squarely at Thomas' head, and pulled the trigger.

LEFT FOR DEAD

WHEN THOMAS CAME BACK TO HIS SENSES, he was face down in the leaves. All around him, the golden woods were quiet. For just a moment, he could not remember what had happened, but then all the events of the last day came back into his mind in a furious jumble. He then remembered the pistol exploding in his face, and how he reeled backward. Why hadn't he died?

Thomas lay quietly for a few more moments, listening for any sound of the pirates. He could hear nothing but quiet forest noises—leaves rustling overhead, the lapping of the creek water below, trees creaking as the wind moved around them. Slowly he opened his eyes and sat up. The left side of his face was bloody, and several leaves were stuck to that side of his face. Cautiously, he lifted his left hand to pull the leaves off and discover his wound, which was a long gash starting just above his left eyebrow and which extended back past his ear. Thomas concluded that it must not be too serious, but only because he was sitting up. The side of his head felt like it was on fire.

Thomas slowly got to his feet, wobbled for a moment, and then made his way carefully down to the shore of the creek. He tore off one sleeve of his shirt, wetted it, and wiped blood off his face, as best as he could. He then rinsed out the cloth, and tied it around his head. He thought briefly that he was glad his mother couldn't see him. She would declare him a sight, and fuss over him. And then perhaps Thomas wished that she could see him.

Having done all this, Thomas sat down by the bank of the creek, and wondered what he should do. How was Captain Monroe? He could try to pursue the pirates. Then what? He could try to make his way back to the nearest town and get help. And which way might that be? He thought this way, back and forth, for a few more moments, but then suddenly felt very weak and dizzy. Thomas moved up the bank a short space and lay down and closed his eyes. He didn't know it, but he then slept for several hours.

When he woke up again, the first thing he noticed was thirst, the second was how the side of his head was still throbbing, and the third was that the sun was now westering. He made his way slowly back down the bank, and pulled water to his face with his cupped right hand. It took a while to quench his thirst this way, but he kept at it, and after a time, he stood up.

He stared blankly across the water. What shall I do? What ought I to do? While he was trying to decide what his duty was, his eyes were looking at the opposite creek bank, not focusing on anything really. And while he was doing this, a thought crept into his mind like a stray breeze, just starting up. At first he didn't notice it, but when the sun settled behind the trees, and the trees stood out in sharp, siloeutted relief, he suddenly started.

The ciphers! They weren't ciphers at all. They were pictures! After a few minutes, Thomas had it figured out. The lines were upright trees, the x's were crossed, fallen trees, and the o's along the bottom were boulders along the creek edge. Thomas quickly sat down. I have to think.

The map he had memorized could have been anywhere. But the pirates knew something about the general location of the treasure, which is why they were roaming this creek. Thomas closed his eyes and imagined the map again, and then he imagined the ciphers, or rather the pictures. He struggled with this for a short time. He could remember both of them easily, but he couldn't get both of them into his mind's eye at the same time. He opened his eyes again. Not much daylight left.

Looking around, he saw a large birch tree hanging over the water about fifty yards from where he was. The creek bank was overgrown, and so it took Thomas about fifteen minutes to make it up to the birch. Then it took him another five minutes to find a rock with a sharp enough edge to cut a deep gash in the bark of the tree. It was hard laborious going, but Thomas finally managed to get a large scrap of the birch off the tree. When he had done so, he looked around exasperated. The sun was going down. He did not want to wait until morning, but it appeared he had no choice. He walked around glumly, and found a place next to a large oak where he could spend the night. He lay down, and put the birch bark carefully next to the base of the tree, as though it were the treasure itself.

When Thomas fell over backwards, Captain Monroe lunged at Carter, but was immediately tackled from behind by two of the other pirates. There was a brief but violent scuffle which ended when O'Conner knocked the captain senseless with the butt of his musket.

And this is probably why no one discovered that Thomas had not really been killed. The fight distracted all the pirates, and when it was over, with three of the pirates breathing hard, it was easy to glance over at Thomas' immobile body, and all the blood by his head, and assume that he had cut his cable and gone out to sea.

One of the pirate chuckled. "Reckon he's gone where there ain't no more pirates." The others laughed, and they all turned back to Captain Monroe, who had regained consciousness, and was now on all fours, looking at the forest floor.

"Pity you took such a liking to the pup," O'Conner said. "But no sense crying now, though he was a brisk young fellow. Let's get on." With that, he nodded at the two of the pirates who had wrestled him down, and they both picked him up. O'Conner pulled his cutlass out and said, "There will be no more of that, see? Once more, and you will have two feet of steel amidships." In reply, the captain just glared at him, but offered no more resistance. O'Conner then turned to Carter, and said, "And no more shooting prisoners without my leave, see?" When Carter sullenly nodded, O'Conner turned away.

"It is either this creek, or the next one north," O'Conner said. "We will work both banks here today, and the next creek tomorrow, and then backtrack our way to the ship before James sends out another party to find our lazy carcasses."

With that, the band of pirates slowly made off, forcing Captain Monroe with them, and leaving Thomas lying on the forest floor behind them.

The sun woke Thomas up, and he lay quietly for a time, not caring where he was. After a few minutes, he opened his eyes lazily and looked down at his feet. Birch bark. He lurched into an upright position. After another minute or so, he stumbled to his feet and made his way back down to the creek. Creek water for breakfast is thin commons. But he was too excited to be too worried about it.

Thomas soon found a stick and a small patch of mud near the waterline, and carefully drew out the picture of lines, x's and o's on the birch bark. When this was done, he laid it out on the ground and stood back to consider it. He would look at the picture, and then close his eyes to imagine how the map had been. Then he would open his eyes again, and look at the lines he had drawn. There were two x's, one over the other, that greatly occupied his attention. On the map there had been some curious lettering on what Thomas had previously assumed to be an inlet or creek, but which he now knew to be a thick wooded point. The lettering had said rex maris. The x in the rex was slightly larger than the other letters. He now saw that the letters were on the point, and that the x was right by the north shore.

The two x's in the picture must line up where the treasure is as seen from the opposite shore, and the x on the map must show where along the creekbank to look for the crossed trees. Should he head back for the river, or up to the head of the creek? Thomas closed his eyes to imagine the map again. The creek was still wide where Thomas was, and the rex maris had been toward the end of the creek. He decided to work his way up the bank.

It was painstaking work. Thomas would walk about twenty yards, and then stop and gaze at the opposite bank, looking for two x's, one over the other. After several hours of this, Thomas started to question what he was doing. What had seemed so clear to him earlier was now starting to seem like a vain bit of daydreaming. He was starting to get irritable, when his eye caught some crossed trees on the upper bank. He could not see down next to the shore, and so he started to scramble along the bank.

When he got opposite the place, he stopped, licked his lips, prayed and looked across the water. There, right at the edge of the water, were two trees forming an x. He looked up above and the trees he had seen originally were still there. He closed his eyes, opened them again, and was sure he had found what the pirates were looking for.

Thomas turned around to get up away from the creek edge to make his way around to the other side unimpeded. The bracken and overgrowth near the water made walking there a hard business, but as he turned, he suddenly stopped. How would he find that place once he was over there?

After some thought, he tore off his other sleeve, and tied it to a branch that would be easily visible from the other side, and then scrambled up the bank to find a path. Once he was away from the water's edge, he was able to make good time, and within an hour he found himself walking along a path fifty yards above the creek. He rounded the end of the creek, and at regular intervals he could see the shore where he had been, and up ahead he could barely make out his abandoned sleeve.

Thomas could feel his heart throbbing in his chest, and he did not know if it was because of excitement, the hard walk, or both. He was very excited.

When he came even with the tattered white flag across the way, he stopped and looked up. Two trees formed an x against the blue sky., with the base of both trees down over the edge of the slope. Thomas stepped off the path, and slid down the hill. When he came to the base of the tree on the right, he saw with excitement that it had been felled with an axe. This was no coincidence.

He decided that he would work his way down to the second x very carefully. He did not know if the treasure would be found in between the two x's, or below the second one, or some other way. One x would have been easy.

Even though he was taking it slow, he got down to the second x soon enough. These had been chopped as well. But they were right at the creek edge, there was no room for anything past them. Thomas walked over to stand in between the two trees, and turned around and looked back up the hill. From where he was standing, he could see the upper x, and so he looked carefully over the ground he had just traveled.

About half way back up, Thomas saw a cluster of rocks, and there was nothing else but leaves and acorns. That had to be it. He walked slowly up to the rocks, trying to stare at them the entire time. As he came closer, he saw a narrow slit, invisible from above, and barely visible from below. Inching closer, Thomas came up and reached out a hand and pulled a small boulder away from the slit. A wider hole appeared, and Thomas felt a cold breeze on his face. It was a cave, and Thomas suddenly felt a cold breeze in his stomach. He pulled more rocks away, and in a moment there was a hole in front of him barely large enough for him to crawl through. He stood outside the cave mouth with his chest full of panic, and rocked back and forth from one foot to the other. Two things occurred to him— the first was that the treasure would take care of his mother for the rest of her life. The second was that the longer he stood and thought about it, the harder it was going to be. But he had no light. But he could still go as far as the daylight would take him, and so Thomas swallowed twice, dropped on his belly and slithered in.

Once he was inside, he stopped for a moment to let his eyes adjust. He could make out the cave floor sloping before him, downward. He wriggled down, head first, stopping every few seconds to look back at the entrance. The cave roof in the meantime had receded away from him, making it possible for him to get up on all fours. This he did, and crawled further in. It was getting harder and harder to see. Suddenly the floor leveled out, and Thomas bumped into something. He felt it and concluded it was a chest, like a large sea chest. He could still see the cave entrance, and so he felt confident in creeping forward a little further. Soon he bumped into another chest, and then another.

He tried the lid on each of them, but they were all secured with a lock. He felt around in the dark and found a loose rock, and he started to bash a hole in the lid of the first one he had come to. The chest was sturdy, and he could not see what he was hitting, and so it was a long, slow business. But he was determined, and eventually he could feel the wood splintering with his left hand. Finally, he had made a hole a little larger than the size of his hand in the top, and slowly he started to reach down inside. What if it was filled with bones? He jumped, and pulled his arm out and sat in the dark for a minute. And why would it be filled with bones? Pirates bury treasure. They don't kill people and then make maps of where they hid the bodies. And other pirates don't go on a frantic search for the victims of other pirates.

And so Thomas reached down the hole again, and his hand closed as soon as he could feel anything. Whatever it was, it felt like gravel and was hard and cold. Thomas quickly picked up two objects in his hand; one felt like a smooth rock or pebble. The other was clearly a coin, a heavy coin. He was breathing hard with excitement, and very carefully pulled his arm out, put both objects in his pocket, and then began to crawl back out toward daylight.

When he came to the entrance of the cave, he stopped. The floor was slanted in such a way that made it easier to back out of the cave.

So he crawled out backwards, feet first, into bright daylight, feeling like a great bumblebee inching backwards out of a great golden flower. He blinked several times, and then pulled the objects out of his pocket. One was a smooth opal, and the other was a Spanish gold piece, a piece of eight. Treasure! At least three chests full of it!

Thomas laughed out loud, and he wasn't sure why. Was it because he had conquered a dark cave? Or that he had found a treasure? He cheerfully decided that both reasons would do, and then thought that this is what it must feel like to be born. Then suddenly he sat down on the forest floor to think. Should I take some treasure with me? Rubbing his face with his hands, he finally decided to leave the treasure where it was. There was no way to manage the weight of the treasure. Better some of a pudding than none of a pie. He would take what he had as proof—if he needed it—and memorize carefully where he was. He quickly rose to his feet and placed the rocks back over the cave entrance.

When he was done, he stood facing uphill noting the location of every rock and bush, and then he did the same thing facing the creek. He still had the markers of the crossed trees of course, but he did not want to risk anything. Trees can fall. When he was done, he scrambled gladly up the hill. In a few moments, he was back on the path, and he had to decide which way he was to go. After a few minutes thinking over it, he decided to continue heading vaguely north, along the portion of the path he had not yet traveled. He would try to count the number of creeks until the next settlement or town, and when he reached that town, he would try to get help for Captain Monroe. But he could not imagine how anyone would be able to help. It had already been a day since their separation.

He was walking steadily, with his head down, mumbling to himself about what he was going to say to the first townspeople he came to, when a clammy feeling came over him. He did not know why, but he stopped and took the opal and coin out of his breeches pocket and thought for a moment. If he put them in his shoe, he would have trouble walking. He started to put them back in his pocket, but stopped again. He still felt the same way, and so suddenly, on impulse, he reached up and tucked both of them into the shirtsleeve he had tied around the gash on the side of his head.

As soon as he had done so, he continued walking, feeling much more comfortable, and thinking alternatively about Captain Monroe and about the treasure. And this is what he was doing when he walked around a bend in the path and strode into the arms of a very surprised pirate.

STILL HUNGRY

THOMAS WAS AS ASTONISHED AS THE PIRATES WERE, and in the middle of the line a glad shout came from Captain Monroe. "Thomas! You are alive!" Thomas greeted the captain, truly glad to see him, but he still wished, somewhat glumly, that he had kept a sharper lookout.

O'Conner walked slowly up to the head of the column of pirates and said, "Well, lookee 'ere. Shot in the head and left for dead, and here ye turn up looking as proud as a pump with two spouts! Carter!" he roared, turning around. "You couldn't hit the ground with your hat!" All the pirates laughed and shouted their approval, and Carter stood near the back, black as thunder. The rum had all worn off, but it had not improved his spirits any. "I can still finish the work, by your leave," he said, glowering.

But all the rest of the pirates thought the thing hilarious, and

refused to let Carter near Thomas. "A man that was born to be hanged," O'Conner said, "will never be drowned. You would just miss again, Carter."

Since they were talking about shooting him, Thomas felt that he should be paying closer interest to what they were saying, but all he could do was think about the opal and coin in his bandage. They, both of them, felt like burning coals, and Thomas thought that all the pirates were mocking him by ignoring the two obvious lumps on the right side of his head. But the moments dragged by, and no one said anything.

After those moments had passed, the order was given by O'Conner, and the group began moving up the path, back over the ground that Thomas had just traveled. When they had walked for fifteen minutes or so, Thomas began to grow increasingly nervous, like a cat on a hearth's hot bricks. Not only did he have clear evidence tied in his bandage that he had found the treasure, but out of the left corner of his eye, he could now see his white sleeve tied to the branch on the other side of the creek. As far as Thomas was concerned, the sleeve was shockingly white, the sleeve was shouting at them all, the sleeve was the only visible thing for miles around. Surely one of the pirates was going to see it, and ask about it. Surely they would go down and find it, and see that it had come from Thomas' shirt, and then they would ask him about it. What good reason could he give for tearing off one of his sleeves and tying it to a branch? The more he thought about it, the less likely any possible answer seemed.

Thomas forced himself to look straight ahead. As it turned out later, the only one who noticed the shirtsleeve was Captain Monroe.

He had also noticed that Thomas was missing both sleeves, and that only one was tied around his head. And when the white caught his eye, he was able to guess that Thomas had tied it there for some kind of signal. But a signal for what, he could not imagine.

They all walked for about an hour until they came back to the place where Thomas had been shot. O'Conner raised his hand. The place was a good resting spot, and O'Conner didn't seem to care that it might make Thomas feel uncomfortable resting in a place where he had been shot in the head the day before. One of them noticed the blood stains on the leaves, and shouted a joke at Carter's expense. They, all of them, were accustomed to using men cruelly, and were dead to all goodness. But actually, their hardness only served to make Thomas feel grateful. It also made him decide that if any pirates decided to taunt or question him he would be as silent as he could manage. After he decided this, Captain Monroe, who was seated across the path from him, gave him a warning look. Thomas nodded at him, and grinned. He sat down on a log, with a pirate on either side of him, and Carter as far away as Thomas could manage. He felt like a goose twixt two foxes, as he told his mother later.

When the pirate band had first set out from the ship they were all filled with the kind of gold fever which makes men think that finding gold is a simple matter of going out and picking it up. Nothing seems easier than getting rich. Sarah Ingle would have told them that whenever you bend the elbow, the mouth opens. But after several days walking the creek banks, the gold fever had left them, and their mouths had all closed again. Now they were still looking and watching, but with little expectation of finding anything. The sting of disappointment had passed, and the party had over all drifted, in spite of themselves, into a casual good humor. They were several hours from their boat, and from the boat to the ship was a short haul, and then there was rum at the end of it. The pirates were men, most of them, who couldn't think about one thing for very long, and if they ever tried, rum would somehow work its way into their long term concerns. For the moment, they were pleased to rest their feet, chuckling and bantering amongst themselves.

"No treasure at all," O'Conner said. "All swabs, that'll describe ye."

To this the group readily gave assent, and one of them said, "I was born crying, I live complaining, and I'll die disappointed." They all nodded as though this were a piece of great wisdom, and one of the others added, "We must all grow fat on proverbs now. And if excuses were as tasty as blackberries, we'd come back to the *Lady Constance* with our stomachs full."

O'Conner was not in a foul mood, for he had grown accustomed to the failure of their hunt, just like the others, but something of the gold lust was still on him. Or at any rate, he may have thought it wise to pretend that it was—after all he had a map he could use to come back with later. And so it was likely that his zeal was for show. "I still hate to come back empty. Our sacks are as bare as the back of my hand." As the rest of the pirates commiserated with each other, confusing laziness with contentment, Thomas sat quietly, and Captain Monroe just as silently commended him.

The only pirate not joining in the general conversation was Carter, sitting down at the end of the log across from Thomas. He was quietly chewing the cud of grief and inward pain. Thomas could not look at him without thinking of something witty to say out loud, and so he made the wise choice to avoid looking at him. Carter was a capable seaman, and a good fighter, and when he wasn't drunk or in one of his foul moods, O'Conner would lean heavily on him. Even Captain James had depended on him from time to time. But there was no talking to him now; he just sat glowering. The events of the previous day were still rankling him, and the refusal of the other pirates to do anything but laugh about it made him a sore man indeed. But if he had known the rest of that day's events, he would have taken a little better care in tending to soul concerns.

The pirate to Thomas' right leaned over and whispered across him to the fellow at his left hand. "Look at Carter," he said. "His mood is as black as the devil's knitting bag." The other pirate laughed, and answered back, with Thomas trying to look as though he was not involved in the conversation. He did not think Carter could hear anything, but the gash in his head made him cautious.

And thinking about the wound made him think again about the gold piece and jewel in his bandage. As he thought about it, he did not know whether to be afraid of their plight, or excited about the wealth he had found, or both.

O'Conner spoke up again. "Mates, when we are done resting our bones, we needs head back to the ship like we had a following sea. When the sun goes down, I'll not be here holding the bitter end."

Thomas began to think that if he kept silent, he and the captain stood a good chance of getting away free. And the pirates were going to release them at some point if they kept to their plan. And so Thomas continued to keep his own counsel. And before long, O'Conner gave an order and they all stood up again.

A RAPPAHANNOCK BATTLE

THE BAND MADE ITS WAY UP THE SOUTHERN BANK of the wide creek, a bank which sloped gradually down to the water's edge and was covered in the oak leaves and acorns of autumn. The rains had not yet started, and so the leaves reflected golden light in quiet peace. It was now late-afternoon and the sunlight slanted down through the trees, which were spaciously arranged, and not at all clustered together. All along the beams of sunlight, gnats moved silently, unaware of the excitement down below them.

Thomas was in the middle of the pirates, and was far enough behind Captain Monroe that talking was impossible. But even if they had been close enough to speak, their pace would have made speaking very difficult. Thomas wondered what the captain was thinking, and whether it was possible for him to have any plan at all.

The pirates were now spread out in two columns, with several of them in the middle watching the prisoners from behind, and prodding them occasionally with the butt of a musket. Despite the late day of autumn, O'Conner's face was beaded with sweat. "They had no time to dig," he remarked. "No time. It has to be in some sort of cave." At his command, the men in the column farther down the downward slope would occasionally trot down the hill further in order to peer at small gullies for any sign of disturbance in the leaves, or some kind of cave entrance.

"How long do we do this?" someone asked. The pirates were all breathing hard, and the backs of their grimy homespun shirts were damp with sweat.

"Shut it, lads. You'll run to the mountains and back when I tell you. Don't you boys want a little bit of treasure?" "No," one of them muttered. "What I want is a spot of rum."

Thomas saw the captain looking occasionally at the sun, and thought he must be calculating the time for daylight left. Thomas tried to do the same thing, but didn't think he could do it as well as any of the experienced sailors there. Still, he thought there must be several hours left—finding their way back to the longboat after dark would be an ordeal.

Suddenly O'Conner stopped and raised his left hand. The band behind him staggered to a stop. Thomas craned to look ahead, and what he saw changed the nature of all of his worries. About thirty yards ahead of them was a solitary Rappahannock brave. He simply stood there, his bow laid across the crook of his left arm.

The pirates stood, whispering among themselves. O'Conner stood and stared at the warrior, but hissed for one of his best fighters to join him. "Carter!" In spite of all the events of the last several days, Thomas thought to himself it was probably because Carter was the least stupid of a stupid lot. Carter walked quietly up and stood alongside O'Conner. Carter whispered, "Can you see if he has the paint on?"

O'Conner shook his head, and muttered an oath. "He is standing in shadow. If he has the paint on, then he cain't be alone. But if he is hunting . . ."

Carter replied, "See here . . . if he is hunting, he wouldn't stand there looking at us. There must be others."

"How many others though?"

"We should try him, see what he might do. Walk straight at him, then stop again."

"No, not yet." O'Conner said. "When we were at that tavern down the coast a fortnight ago, was there any talk of Indian trouble?"

"I don't remember nothing," says he.

Thomas stared at the back of O'Conner's neck and wondered at the strange fate that put his safety under this man's wisdom. After another silent moment, O'Conner decided to greet the warrior in order to try to parley. He stepped out in front of their small band, lowered his musket till it rested on the ground, and raised his right hand. "Hoy!" With that the brave turned quietly around and disappeared into a cluster of bracken.

Visibly shaken, O'Conner gave an order, and the pirates circled, facing out, their backs to one another. O'Conner glared at the prisoners, and gestured them into the middle. Captain Monroe and Thomas stood there for a few moments, hands still tied in front of them. Thomas kept trying to swallow, but his tongue was getting in the way. He hoped that Captain Monroe couldn't see his fear. He thought of his mother, not for the first time since his adventures had started. She still thinks I am on a sloop sailing to Jamaica to sell tobacco.

"O'Conner." It was Captain Monroe.

"What d'ye want?"

"You have two extra hands here. If you can spare two cutlasses, we can help if it comes to a fight."

O'Conner turned his shrewd ferret face around, still glistening with sweat. "D'ye take me for a fool then?"

"Not at all. May I speak freely?"

O'Conner nodded. Captain Monroe said, "Thomas and I would escape from you any honest chance we get. We want to be free, sure enough. But being free has certain conditions on it, and staying alive is one of them. I give you my word that if we come through a battle with the Indians, we will give our cutlasses back to you without a fight, and look for our freedom another way."

"Your word!" O'Conner was still staring at where the solitary brave had disappeared. He spat on the ground.

"Don't take me for a fool," Captain Monroe said. "We are likely surrounded by Indians. Do you think I would take a cutlass and start a fight with you just now? And besides, wasn't it your plan to set us free at some point here?"

O' Connor stood silent another moment, then gave an order, and Carter stepped forward and undid their bands with a dirk he had in his belt. The brown rope had been tightly fastened to their wrists, and when they were free, Thomas and the captain stood quietly rubbing their wrists for a few moments. Carter walked around the pirate band and came back to them with two pistols and two cutlasses. Without ceremony or comment, he handed the weapons over. The captain nodded to Thomas, and they stepped up to join the pirate line. Thomas was facing uphill, away from the creek. He felt better with a cutlass and pistol—just as frightened, but far less helpless.

O'Conner gave another command, and the group began to move slowly and awkwardly back in the direction of the creek mouth. It had taken them an hour and a half to get to this place at full stride. Thomas licked his lips nervously. How long would it take to get back with them trying to keep watch in every direction? Instead of walking straight on, some of them were sidling, a few were walking backwards, and those in front were walking slowly, looking carefully around.

As they walked, their nerves grew more and more frayed. The woods around them were quiet, and the gnats continued to meander all over their straight golden road oblivious to all human concerns. The men continued on this way for the space of a quarter hour, and they began to hope, most of them, that the warrior had simply been hunting deer, and had returned to his task.

Just as the spirits of the band had begun to improve, the woods were filled with a single scream, like a hog being butchered. The wail went on and on for a long moment until it trailed off into a hellish sort of howling. Thomas went weak at the knees, and he could feel the color going out of his face. A moment later, the faint echo of the scream came back over from the opposite side of the creek. The captain leaned over to Thomas. "Courage, lad," he whispered. "This may be your time to become a man. You know how to fight, I know, but deep blood is different than blood from the nose. Let's watch out for each other." Thomas nodded.

The small group of men had clustered closer together, and they continued on, knowing they were going to be attacked, and looking for a small mound of earth or group of fallen trunks to defend. A heavy bee buzzed by his head, so Thomas shook it violently, and stood baffled a moment later when Carter fell over with an arrow through his throat. The captain grabbed Thomas by the shoulder and pushed him down till he was kneeling behind a tree, looking up the hill. They all crouched this way, waiting for what seemed an hour. But Thomas looked at the sun again and realized it had could only have been a few minutes.

"O'Conner." It was the captain again. There was a brief growl, which Captain Monroe took as an invitation to continue. "If we stay here and wait for dark, we have a chance. If we walk in the daylight, they can just start sending your men off to hell like your poor Carter, gone off to join other wicked men. But if they see us settling in here, they will attack to keep us from getting to sundown when we can try to slip away."

O'Conner started to nod but before he had a chance to fully agree, the war screams began again, this time from multiple places. Some even came from below, down toward the creek. O'Conner looked around at the men. For all his cruelty and avarice, he was brave enough. "I will cry fire twice. Baker, Smith, Hawkins, Cooper, Jonas, you fire the first round. For the rest of you, I will wait till they are hard to miss, you can lay to that."

About ten minutes later, as they stared out into the woods, tense and ready for anything besides more waiting, the attack finally began. Arrows began to whir by them, coming alongside the slope lengthwise—from both directions. Thomas thought he saw a snake dart through the leaves, but then he realized it was an arrow. The screams were coming from uphill, and a line of about twenty braves appeared running down the slope toward them, tomahawks in hand.

"Fire!" O'Conner roared. A musket fired near Thomas' head, and other puffs of smoke appeared around the small, huddled group. About three Indians pitched forward into the leaves, but the rest did not slow their howling attack at all.

Thomas pulled his pistol out of his belt. The captain shouted at him, "Don't use that until they are really close. Use it once, and go to the cutlass." Thomas nodded and prayed he would fight well. He thought briefly that he didn't know how to pray any better than he knew how to fight.

Thoughts were coming into his mind with unusual vividness. I am going to kill a man now, he thought, and raised the pistol. He saw off to the side that Captain Monroe had done the same. They waited until the line of Indians was about ten yards away. "Fire!" O'Conner yelled again. Thomas fired his pistol, and saw the warrior he was aiming at stumble and fall. Then everything disappeared in a cloud of smoke and confusion, and a moment later the Indians were on them out of

the smoke, and then the fighting was hand to hand. Thomas scrambled to his feet, as the others had done, cutlass in his right hand. One of the braves was facing away from him and Thomas slashed at his tomahawk hand from behind. He wasn't sure he hit anything, and he realized he didn't know how to fight with a cutlass.

Thomas turned quickly the other way, and fell over backward as one of the braves threw himself on top of him and raised his tomahawk. Thomas desperately grabbed at his arm with his left hand, but the warrior's skin was oiled and his hand slipped off. He couldn't move his right arm with the cutlass. Suddenly, mercifully, the Indian fell sideways off him, his head divided in two. Captain Monroe pulled Thomas to his feet. "Here—stand back to back!"

As they did, they could see immediately how the battle was going. The arrows had stopped once the close fighting was joined, and the gunfire had brought the number of the contending bands about even. About seven Indians lay motionless on the ground, and about three of the pirates, not counting Carter. For a moment the fight drifted away from the two.

O'Conner was still fighting, and the remainder of his men were near him, about twenty feet from Thomas and Captain Monroe. The way was clear for the two prisoners to run off, and take their risks with the archers, however many of them there were. Captain Monroe and Thomas looked at each other, without having to say anything.

"I gave my word," Captain Monroe said, and threw himself back into the fight. To a pirate, thought Thomas, and followed him.

Pirates are evil men, but it is important to acknowledge they are good at some things. They are very capable fighters. The Indians had been on the warpath, but they had been looking for settlers—men who farmed for a living, and who fought occasionally in self-defense. In this band of pirates, they encountered men who fought for their livelihood, and their manner of fighting was not too civilized either.

The battle lasted for another five minutes, and ended when one tall brave, most probably their leader, fell to the ground and was quickly killed by O'Conner. One of the other pirates had slashed his legs from behind at the knees, and when he fell, and even before O'Conner finished him, the other warriors ran off.

The remaining men stood without a word, breathing heavily. "Murdering heathen," said someone finally, a man named Hawkins. Said the pirate, thought Thomas. There were six of the pirates left, and Thomas, and Captain Monroe. "Shall we go?" said the captain, and O'Conner nodded. "I'll be hanged if we stay here."

There were more Indians they had not yet seen, the ones who had been shooting the arrows, plus the braves who had retreated, but in the aftermath of the immediate battle, there was no sign of any of them. There couldn't have been many all together. Maybe with their leader killed, they decided they had to alter their course. Whatever the reason, the Indians had all disappeared.

As they walked along, the excitement of Thomas' first battle quickly faded. He felt a tremor in his arms, and he looked down at his left hand. His right arm was steadied by the weight of the cutlass, but his left hand was shaking in a way he did not believe was possible.

The sun was lowering, and the shadows of the trees stretched a long way ahead of them. After the heat and sweat of battle, the early evening brought a quick chill. The distant sky was visible through the trees, and Thomas could see a thin line of clouds above the setting sun. After the bright autumn sunlight earlier, the sunset was understated, and the clouds looked like the inside of a faded oyster shell.

Although they walked briskly, the sun was soon down, and the twilight was long advancing when they came near the mouth of the creek where they had left the boat.

"O'Conner," the captain said, and O'Conner, who had been at the head of the column, turned around.

"I gave you my word," the captain said, and he took his cutlass and offered it to the pirate leader, hilt first. Thomas followed him a step behind, and did the same. O'Conner looked at the two of them, and shook his head. "Well, if that ain't faith enow."

"I'll put one to that," said one of the other pirates. "They both fought like they was your lads." O'Conner just stood there a time. Then he said, "Tain't natural for a pirate to take a man's sword that way. You can come with us in the longboat now, or you can take your chances here."

Captain Monroe bent his head gratefully. "As much as we enjoy your company, O'Conner, I believe we want to stay here."

O'Conner bowed, a mock attempt at an inscrutable gallantry that some pirates cultivated, and turned to his remaining men. "I didn't want to see the color of their insides anyhow. All hands down to the boat."

"Ay, ay," one of them said, and with that, the pirates scuttered down the sloping hill, kicking golden leaves as they slid down toward the lapping water.

Captain Monroe and Thomas stood on a rock at the top of the hill, and they quietly watched the dark water below through the trees. After a short time, they heard splashing and the creak of oars echoing off the water. Finally, the captain pointed silently, and they both could see the shadow of a boat pulling out to the mouth of the creek. Then he turned to his young companion. "Always keep your word, Thomas."

"Ay, ay," Thomas murmured. And they both laughed.

THE WAY BACK

AS THEY MADE THEIR WAY ALONG, Captain Monroe turned back and over his shoulder asked Thomas, "What happened to your other shirt sleeve?"

"I tied it to a branch," Thomas replied.

"Aye, I saw that. And to what end?"

"The end furthest from the ground," Thomas said, and laughed. The captain laughed also, and Thomas went on. "Captain, I've thought and thought about what to say if the pirates saw and asked about it. There was no good lie I could think up for them, and I don't want to tell you a lie even if I had a good one to tell. I promise I will tell you, and it is important, but I have to think about it first. I hope you can forgive me."

Captain Monroe looked puzzled for a moment, but then nodded his head. "All in good time, lad."

They had made their way several miles back from the shore the night before, in case the pirates changed their minds about letting them go. At the same time, they hadn't wanted to get too close to the place where they had fought the Indians. They found a suitable place to spend the night, and camped rough—not wanting to light a fire, or do anything that might attract attention from anyone. By this time, Thomas had not had anything to eat for several days, and he was getting very hungry. The captain had eaten with the pirates the evening that Thomas was separated from them, so he was still doing well.

The next morning came, and they were now walking along the bank where the treasure was. Thomas almost told the captain about the treasure as they passed the place where he had gone off the path, but he decided to wait until they got back to Annapolis.

"What creek is this? Do you know?"

The captain nodded in reply, and gave him the name of the creek. "When I told the pirates I knew the area, I wasn't lying just to get us on land. I grew up not too far south of here."

"How far are we from the nearest town?" Thomas asked.

"About twenty miles. A good day's walk."

With that, Thomas fell silent, and gave himself to wondering how he would tell his mother what he had found. It was a pleasant daydream, and he walked sturdily behind the captain, well contented with his thoughts. They walked this way for several hours, and took a short rest, and then resumed their walk. The sun showed that it was noon, and Thomas began having trouble thinking about the treasure.

Whenever he would lift the lid of the treasure chests in his daydream in order to show his mother, the chest would be full of pies.

When they had walked for several hours more, Thomas caught a flash of red out of his right eye. He swerved around, and called to the captain to wait for a moment. He ran off the path toward the red, hoping against faint hope. He worked through some bracken, and then, with scratched arms, he found himself standing underneath a wild apple tree. The apples did not look like orchard apples, and were scrawny and small. Thomas had never seen anything lovelier.

He snatched a few apples off the low-hanging branches, and began eating them greedily. He had eaten two apples this way when he noticed a small meadow on the other side of the tree, with sunlight slanting down. The apples over there would be bigger and riper. Captain Monroe stood back on the path waiting for him—he had waved back at the captain with an apple in hand, and the captain had raised his hand in reply, and stood waiting for him to be done with his dinner.

Thomas was looking up at the apples as he worked his way around the tree, and that is why he didn't see the bear. Fortunately, the bear didn't see him either because the bear was busy doing the same thing, looking for the good apples. He was a very large brown bear, and his back was to Thomas. Thomas saw him first, and backed away about two steps when the bear turned and saw him. They both stood silently for a moment. Thomas thought the bear was going to turn away and ramble off, but just then the captain shouted from the path.

"Thomas! You are not that hungry! Bring some apples with you!"

The bear swiveled his head around sharply at that, and then looked suspiciously back at Thomas. He growled low, in the back of his throat and moved toward Thomas. That was all the encouragement Thomas needed, and he shot up the apple tree. He knew that bears know how to climb also, but was betting that this bear wouldn't want to, or, if he did, that Thomas could get farther up and out on to the skinny branches. Thomas was up the tree in a trice, and as soon as he found a high position, he found his voice, and began warning the captain. The bear was circling around the base of the tree, deciding whether to climb it.

"Bear!" Thomas shouted.

"What?" the captain answered.

"Bear!"

With that the captain came walking down toward them, cutlass in hand. When he came out of the brush, the bear turned to meet him, and they stood and stared at one another, just as Thomas and the bear had done a few moments before. The captain then motioned with his cutlass. "Go!" he said. With that the bear just turned around, and lumbered slowly off.

Thomas clambered down out the tree. "Just like the centurion in the gospels. You say go and he goes."

The captain laughed out loud. "That was a bear who likes fruit and berries from the looks of him, and who doesn't like to run too much. All we needed to do was give him an opportunity to save his self-respect. You weren't in so much danger that you needed to climb so high. Come on."

Thomas followed after him. "I was climbing that high to see if I could see our way up ahead. I was being a lookout."

"What did you see?"

"All I could see was bear."

Late in the afternoon, they came to the town Captain Monroe had in mind—though for obvious reasons I am afraid I shan't give you the name of the town. Their arrival created quite a sensation with the town folk, with Thomas' roguish appearance adding to the general excitement. The two told their story to the sheriff, and fortunately, because of their straightened circumstances, the town's one inn agreed to accept the captain's signature for all charges. They got a room to share, and after they had washed, they then went out into the dining room to settle on something to eat. Thomas could smell the beef stew back in the kitchen and thought that he had not been so happy over a bit of food since that afternoon when he had found the apples. He laughed to himself over the shift in the levels of gratitude. But it was all gratitude.

"Did you sleep well?" the captain asked him the next morning.

"I can't remember," Thomas answered.

The captain just smiled. Thomas had talked aimlessly in his sleep that night, and the captain was still wondering about why Thomas had tied his shirtsleeve to the branch.

That morning, they were able to obtain passage on a small sloop that was headed north to Annapolis. Because of head winds, the voyage was longer than coming down had been and the sloop they were on did not help matters by being a heavy sailer. But eventually, some days later, they came into the Severn River, and tied up at the old familiar dock. They had only been gone for a time reckoned in mere days, and yet everything was different. Thomas looked at his hometown with affection, and was very excited about seeing his mother again. The captain had gotten him a new shirt, and a surgeon in the town where they had spent the night had sewed up Thomas' head wound. That was a surprise visit, and it had been quite a trick getting his gold piece and jewel out beforehand, but he had done it successfully. Now they were safe in his pocket again. And although he was still disheveled, he was at least presentable enough to see his mother and not give her great concern.

But before he could go see his mother, he and the captain had to give word to the authorities in Annapolis on the pirates. And since this is also part of Thomas' story, I should tell you something about it. Capturing the pirates, at least some of them, was easier than anyone thought it would be. The *H.M.S. Anne Arundel,* a third-rate ship of the line, had come down from the northern end of the Bay, and had put in at Annapolis three days before Thomas and the captain arrived. When Captain Monroe told their story to the sheriff, he went and told the governor, who then summoned the captain and Thomas to his stately home, and made them go over the whole story again, with Captain Stewart of the *Anne Arundel* present. Captain Monroe told them the outline of the whole story, and Thomas told them some details—about everything except how he had found the treasure.

"Do you know the place where they were anchored?" the royal captain asked.

"I could find it again," answered Captain Monroe. "And we would go with you straightway." Thomas thrilled at his use of the word we, and started to speak, but the captain glanced at him, and motioned for him to be silent. "You do need to go to your mother, and make her happy with more than just news about you." Thomas nodded, and captain continued. "But," he said, "you have no more time than to kiss her on the cheek and tell her you'll be home again safe in a matter of days. That is, if hunting pirates turns more of a profit than a run to Jamaica does. At any rate, be back at the harbor within the half of the hour."

The captain of the *Anne Arundel* was an aggressive, competent, and courageous man, which, when he had first arrived in the Bay, had come as quite a surprise to the Marylandmen. The colonists were accustomed to hardy seamen who wanted to anchor in one or two places up and down the Bay, and who then wanted to attend whatever society was to be had, which, by their Old England standards, was not much. They were in general a discontented and complaining lot, and being assigned to watch for pirates in this distant colony was not exactly a sign of the Admiralty's pleasure. So Captain Stewart had come as a pleasant surprise to the governor, and as an unpleasant one to the pirates, who were also accustomed to excuses for not sailing from the Royal Navy.

Captain Stewart turned to one of his lieutenants, and gave a few orders. Turning back, he said, "They can be getting ready to sail while we finish here." The *Anne Arundel* had just over 50 guns, which is what made her a third-rate ship, and yet it was prepared in just a few hours. A first-rate ship, with over 100 guns, would have taken longer to get ready to weigh anchor. But in part they were ready so quickly because they were not going to sea, but just several days journey down the Bay, and so they were ready to sail at short notice. But after all reasons are given, a great part of the reason they were ready so quickly was their captain's zeal and his disciplined insistence on running a tight ship.

After talking with the governor a few moments longer, Thomas took his leave of them, and ran quickly back up the street to the house where Sarah Ingle worked, astonished the housemaid by knocking loudly on the door, and then astonished his mother in the dining room where she was polishing the silver. After his mother had let go of his neck, everyone there in the house gathered around excitedly as he gave the news about how Captain Stewart intended to sail against the pirates, and how it was necessary for him to go with them. And with that, he gave his mother deep assurances, and ran off down the street toward the harbor.

The adventures were coming to a close, but there were still enough to keep Thomas wondering if he would ever learn to combine courage and caution the way Captain Monroe did. After they came out of the Severn and into the Bay, Thomas found himself standing next to the gunwale with Captain Monroe. "Captain," he said, "why was it right to surrender our cutlasses to the pirates, but it is also right that we are sailing against them now in order to kill them if we can? I don't doubt that both actions are right, but I don't see how they go together."

Captain Monroe smiled an ironic smile, and looked across at Thomas. "There is an answer, lad, and it's a wonderful question. But the best answer I can give you now is to say that questions of honor are not like questions of navigation. And only a fool wishes they were."

Several days later, this is what happened. Some of the pirates escaped by sheer luck. The group with Captain James on the *Lady Constance* had just sailed south from their hidden anchorage when the *Anne Arundel* arrived. The *Prudent Hannah* was just coming out of the mouth of their creek following them. Captain Stewart decided against raking them with a broadside—but this was out of concern for Captain Monroe's ship, and not out of any concern for the pirates currently on it.

The pirates had decided to take both ships down to the Capes a-pirating, and so they had fitted out more than just a prize crew for the *Prudent Hannah*. She still didn't have any large guns, but they were heavily fitted with small arms. The plan had been for them to sail as a consort of the *Lady Constance,* and to use the *Prudent Hannah* for close fighting and boarding until they had opportunity later on to fit her with some big guns.

The *Anne Arundel* arrived late enough to make it impossible for the *Prudent Hannah* to retreat back into the shallow water, but early enough to prevent her making her way after the *Lady Constance*— which showed no signs of returning to help. O'Conner was now in command of the *Prudent Hannah,* and as Captain Monroe had noted before, he did know how to fight. When it became obvious that he had no choices before him, he clapped close upon a wind and sailed straight at the *Anne Arundel* in the hope they could board before Captain Stewart ordered a broadside. But Captain Stewart, in order to spare Captain Monroe's ship, ordered his guns filled with chains, spikes, scrap metal and small shot. The gunner signaled when they were ready.

"Fire!" Captain Stewart roared. When the smoke cleared, the sails of the hapless sloop were in tatters, and a number of pirates were strewn about the deck. Captain Monroe and Thomas were both allowed into the boarding party, and when the order came they boiled over the rails, as ready for a fight as the rest of the sailors, who had seen no action yet. The battle was vicious at the beginning, and to Thomas' untrained eye, it looked as though it could go either way. But Captain Stewart, pacing the deck of the *Anne Arundel,* barking orders to his lieutenants in the boarding party, had a grim smile the entire time. Thomas killed no one in the fight, but he repaid Captain Monroe's kindness to him in the Rappahannock battle. Two of the pirates had backed Captain Monroe against one of the holds, and had fallen upon him in a great fury, and would have killed him sure in just a few moments. But Thomas saw the danger instantly and with one great stroke he took off one of the pirate's arms, the one holding his cutlass which fell to the deck with a clatter. The pirate fell as well, and Captain Monroe dispatched the other pirate. "I'll have to thank ye," he said, touching his hat, "for saving my life."

The pirates fought gallantly enough for a few moments, but when it became obvious that the cause was hopeless, O'Conner ordered their colors struck, and they called for quarter. It was immediately granted, and the pirates taken into custody. They were soon enough assembled on the afterdeck of the *Anne Arundel,* where Captain Stewart paced in front of them, filled with indignation. Finally, he spoke. "I am afraid," he said, "that I will have to bring bad news back to the governor. The best information he could receive was that you and all your crew were at the bottom of the Bay.

MULBERRY PIE

THOMAS HAD NEVER SEEN HIS MOTHER LIKE THIS. Someone who had never met her, like Captain Monroe, would not notice anything, having nothing to compare it to. But for Thomas the difference in her was striking.

Sarah Ingle had always been a matter-of-fact woman. She had been very pleasant, but she was pleasant in going about her business. And of course that business was a hard one, having to support a son without the aid of a husband. Since Thomas' father had died, she had simply given herself over to her duties, and had sought to learn contentment. The small degree to which she had not fully learned it had not been visible to Thomas.

Thomas had invited the captain to come to Reynold's Inn to dine with them the second evening they were back in port. His intent was to have the captain meet his mother, and to have the two of them relate their adventures together for her. The captain had appeared very grateful for the invitation, but when Thomas told his mother about it, she was simultaneously distraught, flushed, pleased, and mildly upset. She touseled his hair, called him a very foolish boy, and said they had nothing to serve but cold pudding and that she had nothing to wear. Thomas did not know what was happening, but decided to keep a weather eye open.

Sarah immediately went to the owner of the inn, and obtained the use of a small, private room for dining, which he happily granted. The owner, a kindly man, then solved the problem of what to serve by telling her that she had free use of the kitchen that night. The return of Thomas to Annapolis, and the reports of how he had acquitted himself while gone, had greatly pleased the innkeeper, and he said that one good turn deserves another. "And Captain Monroe," he said, "what a distinguished visitor!"

Sarah had then come back to their rooms, grateful and flustered, and set herself to the problem of what to wear. She had only two dresses that she wore when she went to work at the mansion, and both of them were quite unsuitable for entertaining company. She then pulled out an old chest from beneath her bed, and carefully went through it. At the bottom of the chest was another dress—one she had not worn for many years.

It was her wedding dress, but now I have to explain something about this to you. In those days, wedding dresses were not like what they are today. It was not uncommon at all for women to buy a good dress in which to marry, but then to use that dress for nice occasions afterwards. In fact, Sarah had done this just like other women in her day. But she had put the dress away after her husband had been lost at sea. She had done this at first for practical reasons—she had not had many occasions to wear such a dress. But as the years went by, her reasons slowly changed, and she now felt that she could not wear it for reasons of sentiment.

She put the chest away two times, but each time, after looking at the other dresses, she came back to it again. Finally, she took the dress out and set it on her bed. She could not ask Thomas about it, and she did not understand her own feelings at all. So Sarah Ingle sat on the edge of the bed for ten minutes or so, and then got up, took her prayer book, and went across the street to St. Annes. She was a prudent woman.

When she came back, she was far more composed and had decided to wear the dress, and Thomas' eyebrows went up when he saw her in it. Like many young men, he had difficulty thinking of his mother as a woman, and here she was, manifestly a beautiful woman. Thicker and thicker, he thought.

Thomas welcomed the captain on the front steps of the inn, and led him back to the private room where they would be dining, where his mother sat, trying to compose herself further. This was difficult because she was already as composed as she was going to get. When they entered the room, the captain took Sarah's right hand in his, and bowed solemnly. They greeted one another very cordially, and

Thomas set himself to watch how they spoke to one another. But he was immediately distracted by the topic of conversation they chose.

"I have to tell you, madam, that you have every reason to be very proud of your son. He is a courageous and hard-working fellow, and on at least several occasions he saved my life. In a calm sea, every man is a pilot. Your son has handled some very heavy seas, some of them mountain high. I am in your debt, for bringing up such a fine young man." The captain was saying no more than he believed to be true, and yet he still felt silly and obvious in speaking this way to Sarah. But Sarah took him at face value, and as the conversation wore on, it became less stilted.

Thomas felt himself flush, and he hastened to change the subject. Since the food was ready, and hot, he thought if they sat down, the conversation would turn quickly to other matters. But as soon as they were seated, the captain began to tell the story of their ordeal with the pirates, from the beginning, and he did not stint his praise of Thomas in anything. If there was an opportunity to commend Thomas for anything, commend him he did.

Sarah's eyes glowed, and her pleasure in hearing how Thomas had acquitted himself was all jumbled up with her pleasure in listening to the captain speak. Finally, Thomas was provoked beyond his endurance and burst out, "Captain, you talk as though I were something more than a very frightened ship's boy. Which is not true! Some have been thought brave because they were afraid to run away." But Thomas was also secretly gratified at the respect the captain showed him, and when the captain told about the fight with Isaac, his mother turned and looked at him with a respect he had

not seen before. "It was not just that you fought," she said. "Boys fight. It is that you had the wisdom to see that you had to fight then."

Once the story had all been told, the conversation moved into quieter waters, and Thomas began to feel more comfortable, and resumed his watch of the captain and his mother. Captain Monroe asked about Sarah's story, and learned how she had come over to Maryland from Bristol in the old country, how she had met her husband, the story of his loss at sea, and how she and Thomas had made their way together. And then she returned the interest by asking for his story—at this, Thomas listened with fascination, for he knew very little about the captain, other than that he was a hard worker, a kind and courageous man, and that he owned the *Prudent Hannah.* He had been born in Maryland, in St. Mary's City, and after a short time at home, he had been apprenticed as a ship's boy, and had grown up at sea. He had always considered his homeports as somewhere in the Chesapeake, but he had tales of adventure from all around the world.

He had fought in the last Anglo-Dutch war in the Chesapeake, and had fought with pirates off the coast of Brazil. He had sailed to Africa several times, and spoke of some of the strange creatures he had seen there. As he spoke, both Thomas and his mother fell silent, asking fewer and fewer questions.

After several hours passed in this fashion, Sarah Ingle suddenly started, and stood up on her feet. "Oh, my word!" she said, and rushed off in the direction of the kitchen. Fortunately, the cooks there had rescued a pie she had been cooking for dessert, and it had cooled to just the right temperature.

When she brought it back, Thomas asked, "What kind of pie is it, mother?"

"Mulberry. Your favorite."

Thomas laughed. "Is mulberry your favorite, captain?"

The captain rubbed the back of his neck with his right hand. "Well, I have to say that it is now. And I feel like a person of great consequence, being served in this fashion."

"It is our way to thank you," Sarah said. "You have shown great kindness to my son, and to me through that kindness."

Thomas nodded his agreement. "And you never know what kind of treasure you might find if you maintain a close acquaintance with mulberries."

Both the captain and his mother looked at him curiously when he said this. "What?" they said. "Oh, I was just thinking of something I saw some time ago."

PEARL OF GREAT PRICE

THE JUDGE SAT QUIETLY AT THE BENCH, his periwig beside him. He sat upright, solemnly writing. Thomas sat quietly also with Captain Monroe beside him. The judge was doing some final scritching with his quill pen, and was deep in furrowed musings. A late summer humidity filled the air of the Maryland court room.

After a few moments, the judge stopped, picked up his wig and put it on, and nodded to the bailiff.

"Tell the sheriff to bring in the prisoners."

The bailiff rotated smartly on his heel, and pushed through the mahoghany doors. The trial had gone swiftly, with multiple witnesses able to attest many instances of robbery and murder on the Bay, with the petit jury of twelve men listening closely. The jury had not been long in returning a sentence of guilty for all the prisoners, and so the time had come for the final sentence to be apportioned.

The judge had his instructions from the royal governor, who in turn had instructions from His Majesty concerning the plague of piracy in the Chesapeake and within the soundings off the Virginia Capes. No real defense was possible, and so O'Conner and a number of the more notorious pirates, about six of them, attempted none. But Isaac Taylor and another prisoner, a man named James Haycock, defended themselves the way pirate seamen frequently did when caught, saying that they had been forced into it, and participated with the others in the pirate trade only because they feared for their lives.

Unfortunately, there were too many witnesses who had seen them engaged in villainy of various sorts, and of a kind that impressed pirates need not have done. Thomas was one of these witnesses, and told how Isaac said that he was running off to join the pirates, and how he had behaved before the fight that Thomas had had with him.

After a few weary, humid moments, the nine prisoners were ushered in, two of them most miserable, and the rest defiant. Judge Alford cleared his throat, and told the prisoners to remain standing to receive their sentence. Thomas was seated about ten feet behind them, and saw that Isaac's legs were trembling furiously.

"The crimes you have committed are in themselves evil, and clean contrary to the law and light of nature, as well as contrary to the law of Almighty God. He is the one who made the sea upon which both you and your victims sailed in times gone by. And He has commanded that you shall not steal, Ex. 20:15, and He has said also that thieves shall not inherit the kingdom of God, 2 Cor. 6:10. Do you understand this?"

O'Conner and the other rebels stood sullen and silent. Isaac Taylor and James Haycock both nodded. Isaac was nodding eagerly.

"And to the sin of theft, you have added the sin of murder. No less than twenty persons have died in battles in which each of you were engaged. And however you fancy that you were facing them fairly in open fight, yet this know, that the authority of the sword was not committed into your hands by any lawful authority, and so those men who fell in battle against you were doing their duty to King and Country, and consequently, they were murdered, and their blood cries out for vengeance. As Abel's blood cried out from the ground, so their blood cries out from the sea. In response to their cries, the voice of God says in His law, that whosoever sheddeth man's blood, by man shall his blood be shed, Gen. 9:6. Do you understand these things?"

O'Conner and his loyal men were immobile and obstinate still, but the compliant two were still nodding. But the solemnity of the moment, and the hazard they were facing, were both growing on them, so that it was hard to see the movement of their heads. Out of the corner of his right eye, Thomas could see Mrs. Taylor, her face ashen.

"And you must consider that this punishment of death is merely civil, and so does not end your punishment, but merely begins it. Murderers, in holy Writ, have their part in the lake which burneth with fire and brimstone, which is the second death, Rev. 21:8. Considering your circumstance, and your clear and evident guilt, the sound of such words must make you tremble indeed, for who can dwell with everlasting burnings? Do you consider and ponder these questions?"

All the prisoners stood motionless. Thomas could see nothing,

but the judge must have seen some reaction in the faces of the two wretches, for he continued.

"I must set before you the terms of divine mercy, which Scripture declares to be faith and repentance. And do not think of repentance as a bare sorrow for your sin, for there is a worldly sorrow that comes to nothing but death. I will not enlarge on the close matters of such doctrines, for a minister of the Word will visit you in your confinement, and will open these things to you further if you wish. It is not proper for me to give counsel and advice out of the way of my own calling and profession. This may be delivered you more clearly by those who have made divinity their particular study, and who, by their knowledge, as well as their office, are ambassadors of Christ, 2 Cor. 5:20. They are best qualified to give you instructions on the way of eternal life.

"However, having discharged my duty to you as a fellow creature, and as a Christian man, by giving you what counsel I can with regard to the salvation of your unhappy souls, I must now perform my office as a judge. The sentence that the law has appointed to pass upon you for your many offences, and which this court does therefore award is:

That you, the said Jonathan O'Conner, shall go from hence to the place from whence you came and from thence to the place of execution, where you shall be hanged by the neck until dead, and you shall be hanged in chains with your body left to the birds of the air, and as a sign to all who sail in these waters, that the God of the earth and sea is wholly just. And may the God of infinite mercy be merciful to your soul."

Thomas saw which way the wind was blowing, and as the judge worked through the roster of names, he saw the punishment was identical in each instance. He wondered if there was to be any change in the sentences when he came to the two prisoners who were showing some sense of remorse. And there was a change, but not much of one.

"And that you, the said James Haycock, shall go from hence to the place from whence you came and from thence to the place of execution, where you shall be hanged by the neck until dead, and you shall then be mercifully buried. And may the God of infinite mercy be merciful to your soul."

"And that you, the said Isaac Taylor, shall go from hence to the place from whence you came and from thence to the place of execution, where you shall be hanged by the neck until dead, and you shall then be mercifully buried. And may the God of infinite mercy be merciful to your soul."

At these last words, Isaac collapsed in a heap on the floor, and his mother burst into a long, drawn-out wail. Everyone else in the court sat quietly. It took a while, because of Isaac's discomposure, but the bailiff finally escorted the prisoners out, and one of the officers of the court led Mrs. Taylor out after them, still weeping.

When all the assembled spectators were outside the courthouse, Thomas turned to ask Captain Monroe a question. "Do you think the sentence was just? For Isaac, I mean. I know about the others."

Captain Monroe bowed his head, and took off his hat. "Well, laddie, there's no question but that it was just. But I think you are asking whether it was wise."

"I reckon."

"Isaac is a coward. But he is the kind of coward who tries to become brave through becoming cruel. And he has done this at least twice. After you licked him honestly, like any Christian man would do, he still wanted to prove himself a man to the pirates, and not to you. I have never seen a worse bit of truckling in all my days. If the judge had showed him mercy, I have no doubts but that he would be just another dog back to his vomit, as the Book says."

Thomas nodded solemnly. "And it all came from being lazy," the captain added. "For those who are lazy every duty is an intolerable burden. A lazy sheep thinks the wool is heavy."

"Does everything bad come from being lazy?" Thomas laughed.

The captain joined his laughter for a moment, but then said, "In a fashion."

The road beneath them was crushed oyster shell, and the glittering white and pearl cracked beneath their feet as they walked. The crowd had dispersed, and Thomas soon found himself alone with the captain. Sarah Ingle had not come with them—she had no desire to see pirates condemned, least of all Isaac. And she had known that they would be condemned.

"Captain?"

"Aye," the captain said.

Thomas took a deep breath. "Now that you have the Prudent Hannah back, would you be willing to sell her?"

The captain looked up quickly. "Sell her? It took me many years of sailing to buy her. Why sell her?"

Thomas decided to wade in slowly. "I thought you might want to buy some land."

"You thought I might want quit the sea and start farming tobacco? D'ye have any reason for thinking I might want to do this?" The captain's eyebrows were arched, but he didn't seem upset.

"No," Thomas said. "I wasn't thinking about farmland. The land I was thinking of is along the coast, south of here."

"So, you want me to buy some land that you have in mind, so that I can sit on it and look at the Bay? And eat acorns?"

Thomas laughed. "No." He looked around again. "I wanted you to buy the land where the treasure is."

The captain stopped walking, and the oyster shells stopped their quiet conversation in the background. "Treasure?"

Thomas nodded. "I found the treasure when I was separated from you all—before the fight with the Indians."

"You found the treasure, or you think you found the treasure?" The captain had had dealings before with young men with active imaginations.

"I found it."

The captain looked around again. No one was near them. He was silent for a moment. Thomas blurted out, "I am not asking you to buy the treasure for me. What I thought was that if you bought the land, and if I showed you where the treasure was, we could split it, clean down the middle. My mother and I would take half, and you could have the other half." A worried look came into Thomas' face. "You think that is fair, don't you?"

"Aye, lad. More than fair."

A minute or more walked quietly, slowly by. Thomas squirmed a little. Why was the captain silent?

Captain Monroe breathed in and out several times. "You're a sharp lad, a sharp lad. I'm surprised you don't have to carry your extra wits around in a bucket."

"What do you mean?" Thomas asked, confused.

"Aye, we'll do it, mate. But you are making me change all my plans. I thought I was managing my tack well enough, but you have brought in a whole new wind from the south, and you are blowing me back up the Bay."

Thomas shook his head, baffled. "What . . . ?"

"After our dinner together with your mother, I decided she was the kind of woman I might want to marry. Actually, I probably thought that when I first saw her on the dock, seeing you off, at the beginning of all our adventures."

Thomas was grinning widely. "Why is this a strange new wind?"

"She is a wealthy woman now. She'll have suitors all around the front door. You'll have to start going in and out by the back way, like a kitchen puppy."

And so Thomas laughed out loud. "She's not a wealthy woman just this minute."

When they got back to Reynold's Inn, the first thing they noticed was a commotion in the road out front. An excited band of men were chattering loudly there, and when Thomas and the captain walked up, it took some moments to get any information out of any of them. Or rather, they got too much information out of them, all of it jumbled together. The captain finally quieted them down, and asked one of them, a local tobacco planter named Henry Carroll, what the commotion was about.

"The pirates escaped! But the leader O'Conner, was shot down, like a dog in the road."

At that moment, a young red-coated officer came striding by, head down. He had just come from a painful visit with Governor Seymour. He was the one who had commanded the detachment that was escorting the prisoners back to the jail, and it was he who had shot O'Conner down. The interview with the governor was not painful because of any negligence or cowardice on his part, or anger on the governor's part. He and his men had acquitted themselves bravely and well. It had been painful because he hated pirates, and he hated to lose, for whatever reason.

Henry Carroll shouted out to him, "Jacob! Jacob Henry! Tell us what happened!" The young man stopped, and came over to the group, shaking his head. His face was still flushed.

"We were waylaid by ten or more skulks, as bold and big as you please. We were outnumbered, but my lads showed themselves men enough. We took two of them down, and the one prisoner. Another of them was wounded, and the doctor tells me the world will soon be quit of another rascal. Three of my men were wounded, but none killed. And that young pirate, as soon as he was off the horse, showed me the cleanest pairs of heels the world has yet seen."

Thomas felt immediately glad that Isaac had escaped, but then he straightway felt guilty about it, wondering if he was an honest friend of the Lord's justice. Perhaps Isaac would forsake his companions, and learn to live true. But the captain was probably right. So all Thomas said was, "So Isaac slipped his cable. That son of a Dutchman!"

After some time, the agitated chatter died down, and the men began to drift off singly, or in pairs, wanting to get home in order to share the excitement with their families. Soon Thomas and the captain were standing alone outside Reynold's Inn.

"Well, Thomas," the captain said, "shall we go in?"

Thomas shook his head. "No. I think I need to wait out here for a short time." The captain glared at him and tramped up the stairs.

DELIVERANCE

OF COURSE THIS WOULD BE A POOR STORY INDEED if the captain had not married Sarah Ingle. They did marry, and they bought the land where the treasure was, and, since it was hidden so well, they decided to just leave it there. And, as it turned out, there were seven more chests of treasure further back in the cave that Thomas had not found on his first visit. Over a number of years, Thomas gradually took out his half of the treasure and became a very wealthy merchant in southern Maryland. The new Monroe family began the long process of investing and guarding the other half. Because there was so much treasure, they never had to take more than a small fraction, and when they did, they used it to establish enterprises that would make their own way in the world.

John and Sarah Ingle Monroe had three children, and one of them was a boy, Thomas Monroe, named after his older half-brother, and he was the one who began the long tradition of handing down the secret of the treasure. That tradition included waiting until the eldest son came to a responsible age, and then, after placing him under the most solemn promises and oaths, escorting him by night to his inheritance. This tradition continued until the War Between the States, when Oliver Monroe was killed in action while serving under General Jackson. Because of all the tumultuous war conditions, and because his son was so young when he died, and because the papers that contained the secret were mislaid by ignorant executors of the estate, the secret of the treasure's location was lost. But because the wealth had been managed wisely in the meantime, the Monroe family continued to do very well. But much had still been forgotten, and the conditions after the war were very different. As time went on, the wealth of the family gradually declined.

Jim Monroe had saved up a little money from a paper route he had, and one afternoon on the way home from school, he stopped and bought the best flashlight the drug store had. He had been thinking a lot about the things he and his mother had learned, and since he knew the creek banks of their property very well, having played there his entire life, he decided to check out a few possibilities that afternoon. His mother had been very interested in the research about the treasure, but for some reason had been very reluctant to actually go look for it. Jim thought it was because she was afraid of being disappointed, but that was not the case, as it turned out later. So when it came about that she was going to be gone one afternoon to go up to the city, Jim decided that he would go looking on his own. He decided, optimistically enough, that he would need a flashlight for the cave.

Sandra Monroe was actually going up to the airport to pick me up. As I mentioned earlier, I had been a friend of her husband's in the army, and after the war, I had kept in touch with her off and on. I had thought through many things that concerned the three of us, and so I thought I would visit them to see if they were doing all right. And that is how I came to be involved in the story at just this time. It was a very good thing too, because they might have lost all the treasure had I not arrived, and had Sandra not confided in me about it on the way back from the airport. She did not know me that well, but her husband had written about me often, and she needed counsel badly.

The reason she needed counsel was also why she was reluctant to go look for the treasure. Jim was approaching the question simply. "If we find the treasure, our problems are all solved." Sandra was a shrewd woman, and she knew that if they found the treasure, the problems could be just beginning. And a central part of this was that she knew there well might be various government regulations about recovered treasure. What it amounted to, she feared, was that someone who finds treasure might not be allowed to keep any of it. And so she did not know what to do if they found anything. She wasn't sure about the laws on recovered treasure, and she couldn't afford an attorney. Of course, if they found the treasure, and were able to keep it, then she could afford one. But that's what she did not know. And so she was trying to put the decision off, and yet the deadline of paying the property taxes was also looming.

At any rate, when Sandra and I arrived back from the airport around dinnertime, Jim was sitting on the living room couch, in a state of high excitement. He looked as though he was about to burst, and he looked disconsolate when he discovered that I was staying to dinner.

"If it is about the treasure, Jim," his mother said, "you can speak freely. I told Mr. Stevens about it."

"Why did you do that?" Jim said. "No offense, Mr. Stevens."

I laughed, and Sandra said, "It is because I needed help in making a big decision. I think I have read before that if people find treasure, they have to report it to the government. If we do not report it, I am afraid of what might happen. If we do, I am afraid of what might happen. I am just plain worried—we haven't even found any treasure, and I am afraid to."

Jim still eyed me warily, but decided to share his news anyway. "Well, that part is solved, anyway. I found it this afternoon while you were gone. From the description of the rocks we found, and how far from the creek they had to be, I was able to guess where I needed to look. So I spent the afternoon walking the creek bank looking up the slope about thirty yards. There were not many places it could be. At the third possible place, I moved a few stones, just like Thomas did, and found the hole."

His mother's eyes were wide open with glad disbelief, happy in spite of her worries. "Did you go in?"

Jim held up his flashlight in his right hand. And then, pausing for effect, he held up a shiny doubloon in his left. We both exclaimed, at the same time, "Can we see?" Jim handed it over, and Sandra turned it over a few times, felt the weight of it in her hand, and handed it to me. I did the same, hefting it in my hand.

When we looked back at Jim, he had a big grin on his face. "There are still five chests of it in there."

"Oh, my soul," Sandra said, and sat down again. We all sat for a few moments, saying nothing. Then Sandra spoke again, "What are we going to do?"

I spoke up. "The government probably does have laws about discovered treasure. If you announced this in the papers, I expect you would have a visit from them soon enough."

"Don't tell 'em then," said Jim.

"I don't want to break any laws," replied Sandra.

"May I make a suggestion?" I said. Both mother and son nodded. "This is not an ordinary case of discovered treasure. You discovered treasure that was in the possession of your family for a century and a half. It was then lost—as far as knowledge of its whereabouts—for a hundred years. But it was always on your property, and has been on your property continuously. It is like losing an heirloom piece of furniture in a cluttered attic, with it being in your attic the entire time. That means that we can be sure that the normal recovered treasure scenario does not apply."

"Then we can tell the authorities?" Sandra asked.

"I would recommend that you do not," I said. "What I have just said makes sense to my conscience. I am not sure it would make sense to everyone else. It is quite possible that you could make this public, and still get to keep the treasure. But there would certainly be a risk."

"But how can we not tell?" Sandra was clearly distressed. "I can't take five chests of gold down to the bank. It would excite comment. And we need to get some money from it to pay our back taxes. The judge won't give any more extensions. He is the original, peevish old man."

"I know," Jim said. "I went back downtown after I found the treasure because the flashlight I bought from the drug store went dead when I was coming out of the cave. I had just bought it and thought I should take it back, and so I did. Mr. Wiggins was kind enough about it and gave me my money back, and so when I was walking out of the drug store I had both hands in my pockets, feeling the doubloon in my right hand and my returned money in my left. Judge Beard was coming in at just that moment and he said something like, 'Here, boy, you're not snitching gum, are you?'"

Sandra gasped. "What did you do?" The fact that her son was there with her still in possession of his doubloon meant that things had turned out all right, but this did not keep her from turning white.

Jim grinned, enjoying the story. "Well, I showed him my change from my left pocket, and said, "Of course not! Mr. Wiggins just gave me a return for a flashlight.' The judge started to ask me about my right pocket, but Mr. Wiggins started to fret at him from inside the

store. 'He's a good boy, Jonas. Don't you harass my customers that way!'" Jim did such a good imitation of Mr. Wiggins' voice that Sandra laughed out loud.

Jim continued his story. "So I stood outside on the sidewalk, and Judge Beard stood inside the screen door and lectured me for a minute on the importance of respecting the property of others. I said, "Yes, sir," as politely as I could and tried not to do anything sudden or alarming with my right hand. The doubloon felt like it weighed ten pounds in my pocket. I know just how Thomas Ingle felt on the path with the pirates. But Mr. Wiggins rescued me by coming to take the judge by the arm to lead him away. They started to talk about a lodge meeting, and I slipped away. As soon as I got around the corner I ran all the way home."

"If I may make another suggestion," I said, "I would be willing to take enough gold to cover the payment of your taxes, melt it down, drive back to the city, and sell it there. Once the crisis over your property taxes is past, we can figure out a way to utilize the rest of the treasure."

Jim had been sitting quietly. He had been listening carefully to all this. And as he told me years later, my use of the word *we* had not passed him by. But he was mostly upset by what he was learning about the government's rules.

"Do you mean that I can't tell anyone?"

I nodded.

"And if I went and showed off some gold pieces to my friends, the government would come and take it all from us?"

"Well, that certainly is a possibility," I said.

"Then it seems to me," Jim said, "that we are not dealing with pirates dead and gone. We are still in a pirate story. Thomas didn't have any problem keeping the location of this cave from O'Conner. Why should we have any problem keeping it hid from some thieves from the government?"

Sandra said, "Shush, Jim. You be respectful."

Of course, as a veteran it was distressing to me to hear a young man speaking of his government in that way, and I would have said something to encourage him to think a little more positively about it. But I couldn't say anything, really, because on this subject there was at least the possibility that he was right. And, if he was, our modern day pirates would take all the treasure away just as ruthlessly and completely as any of the old time buccaneers. Of course it would be done with the appropriate forms filled out, and no one would have to walk the plank, but by nightfall the money would be just as gone. And so we decided, after talking long into the evening, that we needed to keep the treasure a great secret, at least at first. Maybe later, when the back taxes were paid, we might find an attorney we could trust. In fact, we would probably have to. But for the present, no one was going to call the newspaper.

And so that is what we did. It was difficult to do everything as slowly as we had to, but we took comfort in the advice Sarah Ingle Monroe would have given to us. Always eat your brown bread first.